The Day Joanie Frankenhauser Became a BOY

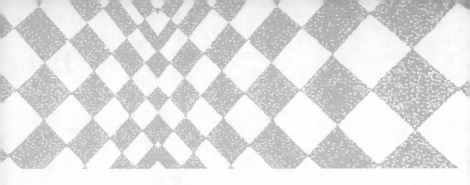

FRANCESS
LANTZ

✳ ✳ ✳ ✳ ✳ ✳ ✳ ✳

DUTTON
CHILDREN'S
BOOKS

THE DAY
Joanie
FRANKENHAUSER
*** Became a ***
BOY

DUTTON CHILDREN'S BOOKS, A division of Penguin Young Readers Group. Published by the Penguin Group: Penguin Group (USA) Inc., 375 Hudson Street, New York, New York 10014, U.S.A.; Penguin Group (Canada), 10 Alcorn Avenue, Toronto, Ontario, Canada M4V 3B2 (a division of Pearson Penguin Canada Inc.); Penguin Books Ltd, 80 Strand, London WC2R 0RL, England; Penguin Ireland, 25 St Stephen's Green, Dublin 2, Ireland (a division of Penguin Books Ltd); Penguin Group (Australia), 250 Camberwell Road, Camberwell, Victoria 3124, Australia (a division of Pearson Australia Group Pty Ltd); Penguin Books India Pvt Ltd, 11 Community Centre, Panchsheel Park, New Delhi - 110 017, India; Penguin Group (NZ), Cnr Airborne and Rosedale Roads, Albany, Auckland 1310, New Zealand (a division of Pearson New Zealand Ltd); Penguin Books (South Africa) (Pty) Ltd, 24 Sturdee Avenue, Rosebank, Johannesburg 2196, South Africa; Penguin Books Ltd, Registered Offices: 80 Strand, London WC2R 0RL, England

This novel is based on a short story of the same title, published in *On Her Way*, edited by Sandy Asher.

Library of Congress Cataloging-in-Publication Data   Lantz, Francess Lin, date.   The day Joanie Frankenhauser became a boy/by Francess Lantz.—1st ed.   p.   cm.   Summary: Tired of gender stereotyping at home, in the classroom, and especially on the football field, ten-year-old Joanie pretends to be a boy when her family moves to a new town, but soon finds there are unexpected consequences.   ISBN 0-525-47437-4   [1. Sex role—Fiction. 2. Schools—Fiction. 3. Football—Fiction. 4. Family life—Pennsylvania—Fiction. 5. Dogs—Fiction. 6. Pennsylvania—Fiction.] I. Title.   PZ7.L2947Day 2005   [Fic]—dc22   2004021589

Published in the United States by Dutton Children's Books,
a division of Penguin Young Readers Group
345 Hudson Street, New York, New York 10014
www.penguin.com/youngreaders

Designed by Heather Wood
Printed in USA
First Edition
3 5 7 9 10 8 6 4

For the grown-ups who made a difference:

my parents,

Frank Griswold,

and the real Ms. Anstine

✳

And with thanks to:

Sandy Asher for buying the original story;

Kendra Marcus for suggesting I turn it into a novel;

Meredith Mundy Wasinger for helping to make the book a reality;

Dottie, Ed, and Christine for the room and the computer;

Lou Lynda Richards and Ermila Moodley for the critiques and the food;

John Landsberg for pretty much everything;

and Preston Landsberg for loving me, even though

I still haven't written a book about machines.

The Day Joanie Frankenhauser Became a BOY

"I'm open! I'm open!" I scream, frantically flailing my arms to alert my team's quarterback, Randy Soworski.

But he ignores me and passes to Chad Taylor. *Chad*, who's surrounded by six defenders and couldn't catch a tennis ball if he was wearing a Velcro suit!

Naturally, Chad fumbles. Then one of the guys from the other team grabs the football and runs sixty yards for a touchdown.

Two minutes later, the game is over, and I'm standing on the sidelines, watching the Mt. Washington School Dance Squad practice on the blacktop. Twelve girls in matching lime-green T-shirts, belly buttons showing, trying their best to look like dancers in an MTV video. What they really look like is elementary-school girls with spiders down their pants.

"Yoo-hoo! Joanie!"

I look up and see Mom waving to me from the parking lot. She never comes to my football games because my brother's games are at the same time. He plays YFL—tackle football with uniforms and helmets. I play flag football—no tackling, no uniforms except Velcro flags belted to our waists—on the interschool league.

"We lost forty-six to nothing," I grumble as I get in the car. "I was open on practically every play, but Randy wouldn't pass to me because I'm a girl."

"Maybe he doesn't want you to get hurt," Mom suggests. She lifts her eyebrows. "Maybe he likes you."

"Maybe he's a butthead who doesn't want to admit I'm the best player on the team."

Mom ignores me and motions toward the dance squad. "That looks fun."

I groan and roll my eyes. "Fun is playing tackle football. Come on, Mom. If Stuart can do it, why can't I?"

"Stuart is three years older than you. Besides, he's got the right build for football."

"Mom, he's built just like me!"

She smiles. "Not for long. You're growing up, Joanie."

"Say it, Mom. It's because I'm a girl. That's why you won't let me play."

"Yes, of course you're a girl," she replies. "What's wrong with that?"

Everything! I want to scream. Just everything.

5:52 P.M.

Mom walks into the dining room carrying a platter of fish surrounded by lemon wedges and announces, "Dinner is served—sole meunière."

Nobody at the table is surprised by this behavior, even though my brothers and I know that most mothers serve hamburgers or microwaved pizza for dinner. But our mom is a junior high school home-economics teacher, and her idea of a good time is sewing, interior decorating, and whipping up gourmet meals.

Dad, of course, is smiling happily, just like he does every night. "It looks delicious, Priscilla," he says.

"Sole mern-*yaaare*," says Stuart, sticking his finger down his throat like he's gagging.

Rob, my sixteen-year-old brother, snickers and says, "Sole of Nike with barf sauce and lemon wedges. *C'est magnifique!*"

I crack up, and Dad shoots me a disapproving look.

Me! Rob and Stuart could make fart sounds with their armpits, and Mom and Dad would just roll their eyes. All I have to do is laugh a little too loudly, and they're on me like a pass rusher on a quarterback.

"I didn't say anything," I protest, but Mom cuts me off with the words, "Kids, your father and I have something to tell you."

Dad clears his throat, which is something he always does before a big pronouncement—like telling his patients they have a terminal illness or grounding us for the next century. "We're moving," he says.

"What?" I gasp.

Stuart, who usually slouches, sits up straight and cries, "Where to?"

"Yardville, Pennsylvania," Dad answers.

"It's got a good mall," Mom adds, sounding like a real-estate agent. "Good schools, too. And it's only about an hour's train ride from Philadelphia *and* New York."

"This sucks," Stuart moans, pushing his greasy hair out of his eyes. Personal hygiene is not one of Stuart's strong points. "I don't want to switch schools."

"What about me?" I cry. "This is my last year before middle school. If I can't go to Mount Washington, I'm not going."

"Starting at a new school is like crossing into enemy territory," Rob says, scowling even more intensely than usual. He pushes a piece of fish across his plate. "Why do we have to leave Boston, anyway?"

"The clinic is closing," Dad explains. "They found an HMO that's willing to see the low-income patients. I could have a job there, but corporate medicine isn't for me. I'm taking over the practice of a retiring internist in Yardville."

"We've had it with the city," Mom says. "We're going to buy a house with a nice big yard. I'm thinking country French interiors, a wraparound porch, and a big garden out back. Maybe I'll even try my hand at canning vegetables."

I can see it now. Mom in her ruffled pink apron, Mason jars spread across every counter, the kitchen filled with the disgusting smell of steamed vegetables. Come winter, she'll be waltzing into the dining room with a big platter of green mush. "Dinner is served—canned vegetables à la Yardville." Blech!

Suddenly, I feel something wet nudge my knee. I look down to see my dog, Amigo, gazing up at me with moist, pleading eyes.

Well, I think, reaching down to rub his ear, *this move is going to be good news for you, anyway.*

Amigo is a high-energy mutt, the kind of dog who chases cats and digs holes and jumps up on little old ladies—and this is after a year of obedience school. That's why I have to keep him on a leash when I walk him. But at the new house, I figure he'll have a big yard to run in.

Amigo lets out a soft feed-me-I'm-starving whine.

"Did that dog sneak in again?" Mom sighs. "Joanie, put him out."

While I'm herding Amigo into the garage, I hear Mom say, "At the new house, we're going to build a dog run. I'm tired of vacuuming hair balls out of the corners."

So much for the up side of moving. There *isn't* one. Amigo is going to be locked in a cage all day, and I'm going to be forced to start the long, probably hopeless search for a female friend who doesn't think getting her ears pierced is the most important thing in life. Or—and this is even more unlikely—a male friend who won't treat me like a girl.

Rob blurts out, "I'm not going!"

Everyone turns to him.

"I'm not," he insists. "We've got a winning team this year. Everyone says we're a shoo-in to take the state championship."

Rob plays football, too—first-string running back on the high-school team. Last year he rushed for nine hundred yards.

"I'm not moving either," Stuart pipes up. "Coach is finally letting me play quarterback. He said I could be starting by the end of the season."

I see my chance, and I take it. "I'll only move to Yardville on one condition—that you let me play YFL football!"

"No!" Mom and Dad shout at once.

Rob and Stuart push back their chairs and stomp out of the room without even asking to be excused. I start to get up, too, but Dad puts his hand on my arm.

"This move is going to be good for all of us," he promises. "You've got to trust me on this."

Dad looks like he needs some reassurance himself, but I don't care. I throw off his arm and run out of the room. In the hallway, I stop and listen. A steady *thump-thump-thump* tells me Rob and Stuart are out in the driveway, shooting hoops.

Normally, I'd join them, but when I'm confused or stressed or angry—and right now I'm all three—there's only one thing that helps me feel better.

This is a job for SuperKid.

6:26 P.M.

I walk into my room and close the door behind me. Then I lift the edge of my mattress and pull out my notebook. The word *SuperKid* is written across the front in Magic Marker. Below that is a drawing of a fist with blood dripping off the knuckles.

The notebook is filled with my secret stories. The first one wasn't a secret—although now I wish it had been. I wrote it last fall after my teacher, Mrs. Pillspring, told us to write a work of fiction. "Let your imagination run wild," she told the class. "Be bold; be brave. Write from your heart."

The weekend before, my family had rented *Spiderman*.

Talk about cool! I loved the way everyone idolized Spidey, never realizing that beneath the mask he was actually shy, nerdy Peter Parker.

That's when I came up with the idea of SuperKid. Once upon a time, she'd been a lonely outcast—teased by the girls at her school, rejected by the boys. Then one day she was doing an experiment for the school science fair, collecting samples of water from local creeks and testing them for pollution. Little did she know that one of the samples contained radioactive waste from a secret laboratory run by the evil Dr. Dread. When she accidentally dropped her bubble gum into the sample, the gum mixed with the radioactive waste and exploded, drenching her with toxic chemicals.

Over the next twenty-four hours, her body developed superpowers. Suddenly, she could run faster, throw a ball harder, and bust bigger skateboarding moves than any human being on earth. From that moment on, she was The Kid—a mysterious superhero whose true identity was hidden behind a sleek red, black, and white mask.

Naturally, SuperKid vowed to find and punish the evil Dr. Dread. She almost succeeded too. But after a bloody showdown, the evil doctor escaped by taking a pill that allowed him to turn into sludge and ooze down the sewer.

When I finished the story, I could hardly wait to hand it in. I was sure Mrs. Pillspring was going to be thrilled at the way I'd let my imagination run wild. Instead, she called me up to her desk and asked, "Are you being threatened by bullies, Joanie?"

"No."

"Then what possessed you to dream up this unsettling revenge fantasy?"

Mrs. Pillspring picked up some notebook pages from her desk and waved them at me. That's when I realized she was talking about my story.

"I—I was just doing what you said," I told her. "You know, using my imagination."

She frowned at me. "This is a very disturbing story."

"Riley McDermott's story is about a ghoul who eats babies," I pointed out.

"Riley McDermott is a boy. Boys go through a gross stage. But girls . . ." She looked at me. "Do you often have violent, aggressive thoughts, Joanie?"

"No," I lied. Actually, I have all kinds of crazy thoughts. Sometimes I imagine I'm a ninja who can kill bad guys with a single kick to the head. Sometimes I dream I can fly. And right at that moment, I was fantasizing about strangling Mrs. Pillspring with the overhead projector extension cord.

Well, the next thing I knew, my parents were called in for a conference, and there was talk of sending me to a psychologist. Fortunately, the whole thing blew over, but only after I'd promised Mom and Dad I would never write another SuperKid story as long as I lived.

I meant it too. But then we got invited to my cousin's wedding, and my mother made me wear a repulsive dress she'd sewn herself. Suddenly, without really meaning to, I was thinking about SuperKid again. Pretty soon, I'd made up a story about the day SuperKid's mom shrunk her special superhero costume in the dryer. Forced to wear a dress, and unable to ride her skateboard properly, The Kid is captured and almost killed by Dr. Dread.

Now, nine months later, I have a notebook full of SuperKid stories. No one has seen them except me—not even Rob and Stuart. I plan to keep it that way.

Quickly, I walk to the door of my bedroom and lean my head against it. I can hear the dishwasher humming and a TV newscaster droning away in the background. I'm safe—at least for a few minutes. Returning to my bed, I grab a gel pen. Then I open my notebook and begin to write.

SUPERKID
in
"Crossing Enemy Lines"

by Joanie Frankenhauser

I was doing my math homework when the phone rang. It was the chief of police. "Superkid, you've got to help us," he said. "The mayor's disappeared."

"This sounds like the work of Dr. Dread," I said. "Don't worry, Chief. I'm on it."

Quickly, I changed into my Superkid costume. I pulled my mask over my face and smiled. Now no one could tell I was a ten-year-old girl. They couldn't tell I was a girl, period. I was The Kid, a mysterious superhero with unreal athletic ability.

I hopped in the Kidmobile and sped over to Dr. Dread's lab, an abandoned warehouse on the outskirts of town. The location of Dr. Dread's lab had been a secret until I uncovered it. Now everyone knew where it was. In fact, just this morning, the health department had slapped Dr. Dread with a big, fat fine for dumping radioactive waste in the creek.

13

Hmm, I wondered. Could that have anything to do with the mayor's disappearance?

I jumped out of the Kidmobile and walked up to the warehouse. Instantly, a mysterious invisible force pushed me back. What could it be? I didn't know, but I was going to find out.

I climbed up to the roof of the Kidmobile. Then I jumped on my skateboard and pushed off hard. I skateboarded across the roof and down the hood. By the time I flew off the front of the car, I was moving at warp speed.

Whoosh! I broke though the barrier! But the g-force was so intense that I lost my balance and smashed to the ground. I shook my head and looked up. There was Dr. Dread, surrounded by his army of giant mutant lab rats.

"This is what happens when you enter Dr. Dread territory!" the evil doctor cried. "Rats, grab him!"

Before I could jump to my feet, the rats surrounded me and led me inside. There was the mayor, chained to the wall. They chained me beside him. "You'll never get away with this," I said.

"We already did," Dr. Dread said with a sneer. "Soon I will announce to the world that I have kidnapped both the mayor and The Kid. If the health department wants to see either of you alive again, they'll drop that fine. Meanwhile, I've built a super-charged ion force field around my lab to keep out future intruders."

I looked around at the dark walls of Dr. Dread's lair. Everything seemed hopeless. Why had I slammed my way through that force field?

I thought back to my cozy, familiar bedroom. Oh, how I wished I was there! Even my boring old math homework seemed better than what Dr. Dread had in store for me.

But then I remembered who I was. I wasn't just some wimpy little schoolkid. I was SuperKid—Superhero Supreme. No matter where I was—on my home territory or in some scary, unknown place—it was my duty to fight evil and save the day.

But how? Then I remembered I had my mini-boomerang in my T-shirt pocket. When Dr. Dread turned away, I managed to lean over and grasp it in my teeth. Using my super-athletic skill, I flung it at the rats. Whiz! It sliced off the general's head! Rat blood spurted everywhere!

Everyone froze as the mini-boomerang flew back to me. I caught it in my teeth. "Free us," I cried boldly, "or Dr. Dread's head will be next!"

Dr. Dread knew he had no choice. "Do as you're told," he growled to the rats.

They released the mayor and me. We ran through the warehouse. But Dr. Dread followed, shooting at us with his laser gun. Zip! Zip! He hit my shoulder. "Argh!" I cried, but I kept running.

The invisible force field was straight ahead. I jumped on my skateboard and told the mayor to hop on my back. Then I kicked off, and we whizzed through the ion barrier at warp speed.

As we hopped in the Kidmobile and drove away, the mayor turned to me. "You saved my life," he said. "But look at you, Kid. You're wounded."

I reached up and touched my bloody shoulder. Then I shrugged. "You gotta be willing to take a few hits," I said, "when you cross enemy lines."

I'm pulling a T-shirt over my head when I hear Mom's voice, all pinched and disapproving. "You're wearing *that* on your first day?"

Naturally, my brothers and I couldn't convince our parents not to move, and now here I am, about to start school at Yardville Elementary. It would be bad enough if it was the beginning of the school year. But no, I'll be walking into a fifth-grade class that's already been together for almost three weeks. I don't even want to think about it.

"That tomboy look was cute when you were little,"

Mom says, "but you're almost eleven now. Don't you think it's time you started dressing like a girl?"

I walk into the bathroom. Mom's makeup is spread all over the counter. Between the clothes, the hair, and the makeup, it takes her about an hour just to get ready in the morning. Not me. I'm like my brothers. I just pull on some clothes and I'm ready to roll.

I gaze at myself in the mirror. I'm wearing skateboarder shorts and a T-shirt. I try to imagine what an almost-eleven-year-old girl is supposed to wear. A skirt? Pink plastic sandals? Come on! You can't catch a touchdown pass in plastic sandals!

Mom appears behind me in the mirror. "Here, let me show you something that would look pretty on you." She grabs a comb and rakes it through my hair.

"Ow!" I yelp. "Mom, quit it!"

Ignoring me, she sweeps my hair back from my forehead and clips it with a butterfly-shaped barrette.

Dad is walking down the hallway, but he stops short when he sees me. "Well, hello, beautiful!" he exclaims. "And who might you be?"

"Stop it, Daddy," I groan. I pull out the barrette and shake my hair free.

"I wish you had a big sister." Mom sighs. "Maybe you'd listen to her."

I shrug and walk into the kitchen. Rob and Stuart are

standing by the pantry, scarfing down Oreos. Rob tosses me one, and I pop it into my mouth just seconds before Mom walks in and cries, "Put those away!" She takes a carton of eggs out of the refrigerator. "Who wants an omelet?"

Rob scoops the car keys from the counter. "No time. You coming, Stu?"

"You're taking Stuart? Drop me off too," I plead. "Please, Rob?"

Luckily for me, Rob has just gotten his driver's license *and* a used Chevy Blazer, so he's pretty willing to drive anyone anywhere. He shrugs, and I grab my backpack before he can change his mind.

"At least wear one pretty thing," Mom pleads as I head for the door. She dashes into the laundry room and comes back with an ugly pink sweater.

"That's yours," I say, wrinkling my nose.

"But it will look so nice on you. It goes much better with your dark hair and eyes."

"Whatever." I take the sweater and toss it over my shoulder. Anything to get her off my case.

Mom looks pleased. "Drive extra careful, Rob," she says. "You don't know the roads around here yet."

"Are you kidding?" he scoffs. "This is the sticks. The only thing I have to worry about is getting stuck behind a tractor!"

Rob is wrong about the tractor. We don't see even one or any farms either. Still, compared to Boston, the traffic is practically nonexistent. What I notice instead is the grass—so green it seems we should be tooling around in a golf cart instead of Rob's SUV. And there are trees, hundreds of them. Tall ones in front of the houses and dozens of saplings around the new condominiums.

Rob turns down School Lane, and there it is, Yardville Elementary School. The front of the building looks a lot like my old school—brick walls with tall, rounded windows and peeling white doors. But the back, where the parking lot is, is much newer, with flat, gravel-covered roofs. Behind it is a big playground and wide fields with more of that green, green grass.

"Don't forget this," Stuart says with a smirk. He hands me the pink sweater, which I had accidentally-on-purpose left on the seat.

I roll my eyes and crumple the thing under my arm. Then I jog across the parking lot and into my new school.

"Ernesto Ardo."

"Here."

I stare down at the floor. It's linoleum, not worn wood like at my old school.

"Miranda Bennett."

"Here."

She's the kind of girl my mother would love. Silky blonde hair tied back in a scrunchy, matching purple blouse and capri pants, white sandals with chunky heels.

"Zane Hamilton."

"Here."

I glance around the room, trying to figure out who I might want to be friends with. Or—since I'm the new kid in a class where everybody has probably known one another since kindergarten—who might want to be friends with *me*. A boy with wavy brown hair and freckles looks my way and smiles.

My heart lifts. I was expecting only the girls in the class to show any interest in me. But it's the boys I'm interested in—unless there's a girl here who's into football, basketball, and skateboarding. And how likely is that?

"Casey Dilliplane," the teacher calls.

"Here," the freckle-faced boy answers.

I smile back and wonder if he plays football.

"Kellie Enderby."

"Here."

The teacher, Ms. Anstine, seems okay. She's young (for a teacher, anyway), with short brownish-blonde hair and a friendly smile. Of course, anyone would be better than Mrs. Pillspring.

"Hailey Dupree."

"Here."

"John Frankenhauser."

I open my mouth, then freeze. Did she say *John?* No, I must have heard wrong.

"Here," I say.

"John is new to our school," Ms. Anstine tells the class. "He just moved here from Massachusetts. John, what city did you live in?"

She *did* say John! There must be a typo on the attendance sheet. The school secretary hit an *H* instead of an *A* and came up with John instead of Joan.

"Boston," I mumble to buy some time. I've got to tell everyone the truth. My name is Joan. Everyone calls me Joanie.

But then I think, *What if I kept my mouth shut?* It's crazy, I know, but the truth is I've always wondered what it would be like to be a boy. Then I could wear the clothes I like without my mom giving me grief. I could write SuperKid stories without my teacher thinking I'm psycho. I could play tackle football like Rob and Stuart.

The way I see it, boys have it easy. They don't have to dress up or stay clean or sit quietly—not the way girls do, anyway—and no one expects them to know how to cook or sew or comfort a blubbering baby. It sounds pretty good to me.

All these thoughts flash through my mind in less than a second. Then I hear Ms. Anstine say, "Welcome to Yardville School, John."

"Thank you," I squeak. "I mean—" Quickly, I lower my voice. It comes out sounding like Shaquille O'Neal. "Thanks."

Everyone laughs, and I feel my face heating up like my mother's pressure cooker. *Oh, no,* I think, as my heart skitters against my chest. *What have I gotten myself into?*

8:45 A.M.

"Okay, class," Ms. Anstine says. "Today we're going to start a unit on biography and autobiography. For your first assignment, I want each of you to find a partner and spend about five minutes getting to know each other. When you're finished talking, you should be able to tell the class at least three interesting facts about your new friend."

Instantly, everybody jumps up and starts shuffling around, trying to pair up with someone they already know. Me, I just sit there, waiting for the dust to settle, so Ms. Anstine can stick me with whoever's left.

"Pick someone you don't know very well," Ms. Anstine

shouts over the din. "*Now*, boys and girls. You've got ten seconds to get settled. One, two, three . . ."

I look up, and there's the freckle-faced boy standing over me. What's his name? Oh, yeah. Casey.

"Wanna pair up?" he asks.

"Sure," I say, amazed that someone actually picked me. A boy, no less.

He pulls over his chair and sits on it backward. And then I remember: He thinks I'm a boy too.

But how do boys act? My mother is always complaining I'm not feminine enough, but suddenly I feel like the girliest girl of all time. My hair is too long, my biceps are too small, and I'm sitting with my knees plastered together like some prissy model.

Wrong, wrong, wrong! I think about my brother Stuart and force myself to slouch. Then I splay out my legs, swallow a mouthful of air, and let out a resounding burp.

Casey laughs. "Nice one. Hey, did you hear about the stupid terrorist who tried to blow up a bus?"

When I look puzzled, he grins and says, "He burned his lips on the exhaust pipe."

I crack up. "What do elephants have between their toes?" I ask. I pause just long enough for Casey to shrug and then say, "Slow-running natives."

Now it's Casey who's laughing. "Hey," he says suddenly, "where'd you score those shoes?"

I glance down at my feet and my heart sinks. I'm

wearing athletic shoes—*girl's* athletic shoes. I begged my mother for boy shoes, but she wouldn't go for it. "The girls' sizes fit you better," she insisted. "Besides, boy sneakers are too clunky."

"I bought them in Boston," I mumble. "It was all they had in the store. My mother made me—"

"Dude, lighten up," Casey breaks in. "I'm trying to tell you I like them."

"Oh!" I manage a smile. "I, uh, I think this style was discontinued."

"You play much football back in Boston?" he asks.

"I was on a flag football team," I reply. "I wanted to play YFL, but my parents . . ." My voice trails off as I realize what I was about to say. "They, uh, they said I couldn't do two sports at once."

"My friends and I play almost every day at recess," Casey says. "No tackling, though. The playground monitors bust us if we do."

"I practice with my brothers," I tell him. It's only a white lie. I mean, we do throw the ball around. "It's like training with the Patriots. Stuart has ten pounds on me, and Rob—whoa! He's a running back on the high-school team."

"You must be good, then," Casey says with a whistle. "I wish I had a couple of brothers to practice with."

"You have sisters?" I ask.

"Nope. I'm the one and only." He leans over the back of

his chair and asks, "Hey, can you teach me to burp like that?"

"Sure, it's easy. You just gulp down some air—it helps to hold your nose until you get the hang of it—and then—"

I open my mouth and out pops a massive *blaat!* Casey laughs so hard he falls off his chair.

"Casey!" Ms. Anstine says sternly. "Would you like to tell the class what you've learned about John?"

Suddenly, everyone is looking at us. Are they comparing me to Casey? Maybe wondering why my eyelashes are longer than his and my fingernails are thinner and rounder? Well, they definitely can't be thinking my chest looks curvier. I'm as flat as Casey. And hips—forget it. I don't have any.

"We're waiting, Casey," Ms. Anstine says as he scrambles back onto his chair.

"Well, John has two brothers," Casey says. "And, uh, he burps real good."

The boys snicker, the girls giggle, and even Ms. Anstine cracks a smile. Fat chance she'd do that if she knew I was a girl. I feel a wave of happiness wash over me. Already my new identity is paying off.

"And," Casey adds, "he likes football. He's going to play with us at recess."

I can hardly believe my ears. Football with the boys! And what's more, I bet they'll even pass me the ball!

"Your turn, John," Ms. Anstine says. "Three things you've learned about Casey."

"He's an only child," I say, remembering to keep my voice from rising like it does sometimes when I get excited. "He knows some really funny jokes, and he loves football."

I turn to Casey and our eyes meet. He grins, and I feel suddenly light inside, like a balloon being pumped up with helium. School has just started and already I've made a friend—a guy friend who doesn't treat me like a dumb girl.

10:45 A.M.

Heading out to recess, the insanity of it hits me. Now it's not just my class I have to pretend in front of; it's the entire school. I force myself to swagger, not walk down the hall.

"Are you all right?" a passing teacher asks.

"What?" I gulp, panic welling up in me. "I mean, I'm fine. Why?"

"Oh, good," he says. "You were walking as if you'd pulled a groin muscle or something."

After that, I tone down the swagger and just concentrate on keeping the bounce out of my step. I notice a couple of girls from my class—Hailey and Kellie are their names, I think—practically skipping out the door. No way do I want to look like that.

I stop at the drinking fountain, which is right next to the boys' bathroom. A kid walks through the door and I catch a glimpse of the urinals. Right then and there, I decide I will never go to the bathroom during school hours, even if I have to hold it until my bladder bursts.

On the playground, plastic cones have been set up to mark off a football field. I spot a lone boy standing on the thirty-yard line, tossing a football into the air and catching it. He turns, and I see his spiky-haired silhouette. He's all arms and legs, skinny and gawky-looking, but when he suddenly steps back and kicks the ball into the air, my mouth drops open. The football flies up, up, and lands a good fifty yards downfield.

A girl standing on the sidelines picks up the ball and throws it back. It wobbles in the air and starts to fall. Like a bullet, the spiky-haired kid takes off running, so fast he's almost a blur. He catches the ball easily and jogs back in my direction, throwing up his arms like he's just made a touchdown.

I laugh. Instantly, the kid turns and sizes me up. Then he rears back and flings the football at me. I raise my hands—more to protect myself than anything else—and catch it.

"You ever play running back?" he asks. "Go on, see if you can get past me."

Now I recognize him. He's a kid from my class. Sits in the back row. Zane, I think.

"What's wrong, Frankenstein? You got glue on your Nikes?"

I've been called that name before, and I've always hated it. But that was when I was a girl, a girl being teased by boys. Coming from Zane, the name sounds somehow different. More like a real nickname, like the way Rob and Stuart call each other Robot and Stewball.

"Get ready to eat my dust," I say.

I tuck the football under my arm and jog toward Zane slow and easy, not giving anything away, just letting him wonder if I've got the moves to get past him. Finally, when I'm almost on top of him, I veer left and turn on the juice. He lunges at me, arms extended, but I do a quick zigzag and slip past him.

"Oh, yeah!" I whoop, putting on the brakes.

I turn to face him, a big grin on my face, and *whoa!*— there he is, running at me at full speed, snarling like a pit bull going after a mailman. Before I can react, he tackles me, throwing me back onto the grass.

Zane jumps up, laughing. It's all I can do to sit up. My chest feels like a playground ball that someone stomped on.

"I . . . I thought you guys played touch football," I gasp. Inside, I'm thinking, *Where's a playground monitor when you need one?*

"Maybe we're too rough for you," Zane says, all fake concern. "There's a kickball game over there. They've probably got room for one more."

Right now that kickball game looks pretty good. But then I remember who I am. John Frankenhauser. A boy. And boys don't back down.

"What's going on?" Casey asks, stepping up behind Zane. He's got six more guys with him, and they're all staring at me. Quickly, I scramble to my feet.

"Nothing," I say. "Let's play some football."

"I've got Ernesto, Spencer, Miguel, and Grady," Zane says, pointing to each boy in turn.

Zane has five boys on his team. We only have four. I glance around, waiting for someone to argue, but nobody does. The guys line up across from one another on the fifty-yard line. I take my place next to Casey.

"Can I play?" a voice asks.

It's a girl. She's wearing turquoise shorts and a sleeveless white blouse. Her thick black hair is pulled back into a ponytail.

"You again?" Zane asks. "I thought we explained this to you at the beginning of the year. This is serious football. No girls allowed."

"But that's not fair," I blurt out.

The boys turn to stare at me. I'm sure they can read the truth in my eyes. I'm not one of them. I'm a girl, just like her.

"Anyway," I mutter, "we need another player."

"Since when do new kids make the rules?" Zane shoots back. "Besides, who says it isn't fair? We don't ask the girls to let us braid friendship bracelets with them."

The boys laugh, Casey included. I laugh too, but it's because I'm so relieved I haven't blown my cover.

Suddenly, the girl grabs the football from Zane's hands. "Catch me if you can," she cries and starts running down the field.

All of us except Zane take off after her. Casey gets close enough to make a flying leap at her shoulders, but she turns on the power and leaves him lying in the grass. The rest of us are at least ten yards behind as she runs into the end zone.

Everyone turns to Zane. Did she change his mind? But he just smirks and says, "Okay, I'm impressed. Keep at it and someday you'll make the track team. The *girls'* track team. Now can we have our ball back?"

The girl's neck is red, and the color is rising like a thermometer in a heat wave. She throws the ball down hard and stomps off the field.

Miguel Rodriguez picks it up and we get back into formation. Miguel hikes it to Zane, who trots backward, looking for an open man. There's only one—Ernesto Ardo. Zane rears back to make the pass.

Then, suddenly, Zane surprises us by hunkering down and charging into the gap. It takes us all a second to figure out what's going on. Then a guy on my team leaps at Zane and misses. Casey runs after him, but he's way too slow.

Now Zane is sprinting past me, on his way to the end zone. He smiles as he meets my eye. "Eat my dust," he snarls.

I remember the way he pounded me into the grass. I remember the fake concern in his voice when he said, "Maybe we're too rough for you."

I put on a burst of speed and overtake him. I throw out my hands to touch his shoulders, but when I feel his shirt against my fingertips, I give him a sudden, hard shove. He flies forward, runs about three more steps with his chin practically touching the ground, and then hits the grass. He rolls twice and skids to a stop. My team lets out a cheer.

I walk over and hold out my hand. I see a grudging respect in his eyes as I help him up. It feels good until I notice Casey. He's eyeing me with a look I can't read. Like I've surprised him maybe. But is that good or bad? Before I can decide, he walks over and holds up his hand for a high five. I slap it and start to smile, but he turns away.

3:30 P.M.

"You're free!" I shout, throwing open the door to Amigo's dog run. He shoots out like a bottle rocket and leaps at my chest, knocking me backward—kind of like Zane did today. As soon as I hit the grass, Amigo jumps on me and starts licking my face.

"Blech!" I scream and roll away. Then I sit up and scratch behind Amigo's ears. He closes his eyes and lets out a deep, low rumble. Doggie bliss!

"Amigo, I've got a secret to tell you," I say. "I'm free now too."

He pushes against me like he's urging me to say more.

"The whole school thinks I'm a boy," I whisper, "and that means I can finally cash in on all the perks."

I'm not exactly sure what the perks are—besides playing football and burping without getting busted—but I'm definitely eager to find out.

"The thing is," I explain to Amigo, "I gotta make sure I don't blow my cover."

Just the thought of it makes a shiver slide down my spine. I think back to this afternoon, when the final bell rang. I was putting my math workbook in my backpack when Zane noticed Mom's pink sweater sticking out.

He was on it in an instant. "What's this?" he demanded, grabbing a sleeve.

"Oh . . . *that?*" I said, thinking fast. "I, uh, found it lying in the hall. I'm going to take it to the office. To the Lost and Found."

"Sure you don't want to try it on?" Zane smirked. "I bet it would look real pretty on you."

I let myself relax a little. Zane had bought my story.

"Why don't you try it on yourself," I shot back. "I think pink's your color, dude."

Zane scoffed and threw the sweater over my shoulders just as Ms. Anstine called, "What's going on over there?"

I quickly shrugged it off. It landed on the floor in a heap.

"Nothing," Zane said. He grabbed his backpack and made a beeline for the door.

I did the same. Now the sweater probably *is* in the Lost and Found, put there by the janitor. That's fine, as long as Mom doesn't remember to ask for it back.

"From now on, Amigo, I've got to be extra-careful," I say. "I can't do anything to give away my secret identity."

And then I start to wonder, *What do the kids see when they look at me? Do I really look like a boy?*

I jump to my feet, eager to check myself out in a mirror, but Amigo thinks I want to play. He runs to get his rubber pull toy and shakes it at me, daring me to chase him.

How can I say no? Amigo is supposed to be the family's dog, but he's always liked me best. I guess that's because I take the time to pet him and wrestle with him. And at night, I let him sleep on my bed—that is, if Mom doesn't find out and banish him to the garage.

"Here I come!" I cry, lunging at him. He takes off running, and we circle the yard a few times. Finally, he lets me grab one end of the toy and we pull each other back and forth. He's got more strength in his jaws than I have in both arms, but eventually he lets me win because he knows I'll throw it for him.

"Go get it, boy!"

I fling the pull toy across the yard. While he's running to get it, I dash to the back door and unlock it. He's there in an instant, slipping in between my legs.

"Okay, okay, you win," I say with a laugh.

I fill his dog bowl and let him eat in the kitchen instead of the garage. Then I head to the bathroom. But the mirror isn't my first stop. I haven't peed all day and my bladder's about to burst!

When I'm finished, I walk to the mirror. It's just me looking back. Just Joanie. But then I try to picture myself the way the kids at school see me. Now I see a skinny, wiry body draped in baggy skater clothes. Okay, it's not impossible, I decide. If you were thinking "boy," I guess that's what you'd see.

Next, I zero in on my face. Dark brown eyes, slender nose, lips that are neither too thick nor too thin. The only thing that doesn't quite fit is the hair. It's shaggy and full, and it hangs over my forehead and ears and down the back of my neck. Kind of girlish, it seems to me. Not that some boys don't have long, shaggy hair—especially skateboarders. But if you were looking for a clue to my true identity, that might just be it.

"So it's got to go," I mutter, reaching in the drawer for a pair of scissors.

I chop at the left side until my ear is exposed. I'm just about to slice off a hunk on the other side when I hear the back door open and Mom yell, "Who fed Amigo in the kitchen?"

I'm busted. But it's not the dog dish I'm worried about. It's my hair. I mean, what was I thinking? I can't cut it off and expect no one to notice. Everyone in my family is going to have something to say about it—especially my mother. And what she'll say is *not* going to be good!

"Joanie, are you home?" Mom calls.

"In here," I mumble.

Mom's moving toward my voice like a guided missile. "Where are you?" she calls as she plows down the hallway. She passes the bathroom and stops dead. Instantly, she spins around. When she sees me, her eyebrows shoot up toward her hairline.

"Joanie!" she cries. "Oh, my heavens, what have you done?"

I shrug. "I'm sick of my hair."

"It looks like you took a lawn mower to it!" She grabs my hand. "Come on, we're going to Cut 'n' Curl. If anybody can fix this, it's Alison."

I take one last look in the mirror. I look like a cocker spaniel with one ear missing. Okay, maybe Mom's right. This is a job for a professional.

"What were you thinking?" Mom asks as we drive to the salon.

She's asked me this like six times already. I guess she doesn't like the grunts I've been giving as an answer. But what am I supposed to say? I can't tell her the truth or even an edited version of it. She just wouldn't get it.

At the salon, we have to wait until Alison finishes with her scheduled client. Mom opens an issue of *InStyle* and leafs through the photos. The models are wearing clothing I've never seen on an actual human being. Plus, their hair looks like it's been curled and fluffed and combed into something resembling a maze of snakes.

I glance at Mom nervously. I hope she isn't going to ask Alison to do something like that to me. But then I remind myself there's no way. There are only about two inches of hair above my left ear. Even the *InStyle* fashion editors couldn't fluff and curl that.

Finally, Alison is ready for me. I sit in the chair and she checks the damage. "What look were you trying for?" she asks gently.

Mom seems to think she's talking to her. "How about a pixie cut?" she says. "That would be cute."

Alison scrunches up her face and looks at me from a couple of different angles. "I'll try," she says at last.

By the time she evens it all up, it's pretty short. The

only pixie-ish parts are the two wispy little curls that she combs in front of each ear.

Mom gazes at me in the mirror. Our faces are side by side, and the difference couldn't be more obvious. She's got big blue eyes, a small, slender nose, and shoulder-length blonde hair.

She lets out a weary sigh. The sound makes my chest feel all hollow inside. I know when she looks at me she'd like to see a miniature version of herself. But that's just not me—especially not now.

"Let's stop at the drugstore," she says. "I want to look at the lipsticks."

I'm feeling so guilty, I don't even complain.

5:25 P.M.

"This lip gloss would look adorable on you," Mom says, holding up a sample tube. "It's very subtle. It just makes your lips shine."

"Why would I want shiny lips?" I ask.

"Because it looks pretty. Come here, Joanie. I'll show you."

She slathers the sample tube across her fingertip, then rubs her finger over my lips. I look in the little display mirror and open my mouth like the models in the magazine. Then I use my tongue to push some spit onto my lower lip. It hangs there for a second before it starts to fall.

"What are you doing?" Mom demands.

I slurp up the spit and shrug. "Nothing."

"Why don't we get this? You can wear it tomorrow."

"Okay," I say because I want to do at least one thing today that doesn't disappoint her.

It works. She's positively beaming as she pays the cashier.

On the way home, she turns to me. "You know, Joanie, fifth grade was the year when I first started to notice boys."

"I notice boys," I say. "I notice they get to play YFL football."

"I mean romantically," she says.

Casey's face pops into my head. Why did he turn away after I tackled Zane today? I mean, Zane is the obvious leader of the group. So if I act like him, that's good, right?

And then it occurs to me that guys don't waste their time worrying about stuff like that. *Does he like me? Did I do something to make him mad?* That's the way girls think. And John Frankenhauser definitely wouldn't be caught dead thinking like a girl.

Mom pulls into the parking lot of the shopping center near our house. "We need milk," she says. On the way into the store, I push my pixie curls behind my ears, blending them in with the rest of my hair.

We're standing at the counter—Mom's paying for the milk, and I'm looking for a price sticker on the football cards—when the clerk turns to me and says, "They're a dollar-fifty a pack, son."

I see Mom wince. "She's a girl," she says sharply.

The guy is all apologies. For Mom's sake, I try to look offended. But inside, I'm prancing like a pro football player in the end zone. My new haircut is an epic success! Now no one at Yardville Elementary will *ever* guess I'm a girl!

6:48 P.M.

I'm pedaling my bike toward the Yardville Preserve. It's a big patch of open land, maybe twenty acres in all, that the city owns. Kind of a park, only nothing like we had back in Boston. There are no swings or slides or park benches at the preserve. Just open space and lots of it.

Amigo is running by my side on a loose leash. It's awesome the way he can stay right beside me, matching my speed without breaking a sweat—or maybe I should say a *pant*, since dogs don't actually sweat. I'd take him off the leash, but the one time I tried it, he chased the neighbor's cat and accidentally clipped a two-year-old. Like I said, he's a high-energy mutt.

Of course, my brothers had a few things to say about

my haircut at dinner tonight. Dad was at a Rotary meeting, so Mom made her version of mini-pizzas—French rolls with melted mozzarella and tomato slices. Not exactly Domino's, but I have to admit they were pretty good.

"You look like Winona Ryder on a bad-hair day," Rob had quipped.

When Mom wasn't looking, Stuart stuck his fingers in the salad dressing and ran them through my hair to make spikes. "Very punk, dude." He snickered. I got him back by stuffing a piece of lettuce down his collar.

Now, a cool autumn breeze is blowing, chilling my ears and reminding me just how short my hair really is. And just how far I've moved from my old life back in Boston. The parks were filled with pigeons there, not hawks. I was Joanie, not John.

It's a lot to deal with, so I turn my attention to Amigo. He's straining at the leash, sniffing the air. I get off my bike at the trailhead and set him free. He bounds into the grass, stiff-legged, trying to flush out a mouse. He succeeds and brings it to me, then drops it at my feet.

Ew! It's pretty gross, but I can't get mad—not when he looks so proud of himself. "Good boy," I say. He wags his tail and trots away, looking for something else to hunt.

That's what I love about Amigo. Everybody else has all these annoying expectations about who I am and what I'm supposed to be doing. *Grow up. Stop dressing like a boy. Be a lady.* But all Amigo wants from me is food, long walks, and love. I can handle that, no problem.

I walk my bike down the trail until it opens up into a wide, grassy meadow. Squinting into the setting sun, I search the fields for Amigo. What I see instead is a boy riding a BMX bike over some jumps. I've seen those jumps on other walks. They're a series of kid-made dirt mounds, perfect for catching air.

I spot Amigo near the jumps and start walking down one of the trails that crisscross the meadow. As I get closer, I think I recognize the BMX rider's curly brown hair and red T-shirt. It's Casey!

He spots me too and squints. "Hey, John, is that you?"

It still takes me a second to respond to that name. "Hi!" I call. Then I jump on my bike and ride over to join him.

"You live near here?" he asks as I hit the brakes.

"Lookover Way," I reply. "You?"

"Crescent Avenue," he says, pointing to the other side of the preserve.

"You look pretty good on those jumps," I tell him.

"I helped build them. There's a whole series of them, from baby stuff to the one we call Mondo Mountain."

"I bust ollies on my skateboard, but I've never tried it on a bike."

"Oh, I forgot. You're a city kid. Well, give it a try. It's not so hard."

As I climb on my bike, Amigo comes bursting into the

clearing like a cheetah chasing a gazelle. Casey jumps back. Then, suddenly, Amigo stumbles and falls, his chest skidding across the dirt. He's up in an instant, trotting toward me like nothing even happened.

Casey lets out a relieved laugh. "I thought it was a coyote or something." Amigo walks over to sniff Casey's Nikes. "Is he yours?"

I nod. "His name's Amigo."

"That means *friend*, right?" He smiles and leans down to pet Amigo's head. "What kind is he?"

I shrug. "There's some German shepherd in there for sure. Maybe border collie or Australian shepherd. We got him at the pound."

Casey looks up at me. "You want to try a jump?"

"Sure."

"This one's good to start on," he says, pointing to a mound of packed dirt about three feet across and two feet high. "You need to get up some speed. Start about fifty feet back and go all out."

I pick a spot I figure is about fifty feet from the jump and line myself up. My stomach is fluttering and my legs feel a little shaky, just like the first time I tried to bust an ollie off the curb outside my house. I wiped out pretty bad that day, but I don't want to think about that now.

I kick off and start pedaling. But my shaky legs aren't pumping as fast as I'd like. Should I stop and try again? No, I'm almost there. There's no turning back now.

Whoosh! I fly into the air with my heart pounding. *Oh, yeah*, I think. *I can do this!* Then I come down and—oh, no! I'm skidding sideways, frantically trying to keep my balance. Not a chance. I hit the dirt, fall off my bike, and slide to a stop on my stomach.

Tears fill my eyes, partly because of the burning pain in my elbow and partly because I just made a fool of myself in front of Casey. Before I can even sit up, Amigo bounds over and starts licking my face.

Casey is right behind him. "You okay?"

Suddenly I realize I can't let him see me crying. Boys don't do that! Luckily for me, Amigo has licked away most of the tears. I scramble to my feet and wipe my nose. "I'm fine," I mumble.

"You sure? I think your elbow's bleeding."

"I said I'm fine." But I have a feeling he doesn't believe me. He's still walking toward me, looking concerned.

Quickly, I hop on my bike and ride back to where I started. Then I go again, pedaling so hard my thighs hurt. When I hit the jump for the second time, Casey is just a blur. I focus all my attention on my front wheel, making sure I keep it straight. And then—*yes!* I land the jump and pedal back to Casey. I hit the brakes and skid to a stop right in front of him, a big grin on my face.

"Sweet," he says. No turning away like he did after I tackled Zane. He really means it this time.

"Thanks," I reply, taking off my helmet.

"Hey, you got your hair cut."

"I got them *all* cut."

He rolls his eyes. "Let me see your elbow."

I twist my arm so we can both look. I've got a nasty road rash. One corner of it is bleeding, and it stings like crazy.

"That must hurt," he says.

I'm not sure what I'm supposed to say, so I just shrug.

Casey doesn't say anything for a moment. Then he climbs on his bike and calls, "Come on. I want to show you something." He rides down the trail, and I follow with Amigo by my side. We're heading toward the north side of the preserve, a part I haven't explored yet. It's wilder over here, with more trees and heavy underbrush.

Casey stops and we both get off our bikes. He leads me to the edge of a cliff. We're looking into a gorge, about thirty feet deep and maybe a hundred yards across. A little creek snakes through it.

"See this tree?" Casey says, pointing to a twisted oak on the very edge of the cliff. Half the roots are exposed. Some even dangle in midair. One branch reaches out over the gorge like a scarecrow's arm. "I've seen Zane hang from that branch by his knees," he says. "That dude knows no fear."

Is that good? I wonder. I mean, climbing such an unstable tree seems pretty scary. And hanging by your knees over the gorge—that's just nuts! But Casey looks impressed, so I figure I should be too. "Cool," I say.

He nods. "Hey, I'm thinking of building a tree house. You wanna help me?"

"In *this* tree?"

He laughs. "No way. There's a big maple over by the Stiegman Street entrance that looks good."

Yes, yes, yes! I want to shriek. Not that I know the first thing about building anything, but so what? The point is Casey wants to do stuff with me. "Sure," I say, trying not to seem too pathetically eager.

Casey looks toward the horizon. The sun is below the treetops and the preserve is turning into one big shadow. "I better go. I haven't even started my homework," he says.

"Me neither."

"See you tomorrow, then." He hops on his bike and pedals away down the trail.

I wait until he disappears around a corner. Then I look down at Amigo and grin. "I've got a friend," I tell him. "A friend who doesn't treat me like a dumb girl!"

Of course, Casey doesn't know I *am* a girl, but that's not the point. The point is I can hardly wait until tomorrow.

Maybe moving to Yardville wasn't such a bad idea after all.

SUPERKID
in
"Guts to Spare"

by
~~Joanie~~ John Frankenhauser

"This is the chief of police," the voice on the phone said. "Dr. Dread was spotted down at the junkyard in the dead of night, stealing all sorts of mechanical parts—everything from broken computers to old bedsprings. I think he's up to something."

"Don't worry, sir," I said. "I'm on it."

I called all my superhero buddies and asked them to meet me at my hideout.

The first to arrive was Zane, also known as the Porcupine. He was tough as nails, with an attitude to match. And when he threw his deadly quills, watch out!

The next to show up was Ernesto, also known as the Blade. His hands could turn into knives, and his feet could transform into hatchets.

Next came Spencer, aka Slime Boy. When he spit, bullets of slime flew out of his mouth, knocking his opponent to the ground and bathing him in deadly ooze.

The last to arrive was Casey, aka Toolbox. His body had been fitted with dozens of amazing tools—everything from hammers to power drills to circular saws. He could use his tools to create or—if he was attacked—to destroy.

"I need your help," I told them. "I want to create a team of superheroes to help me battle Dr. Dread. We'll call ourselves the League of SuperDudes. Are you with me?"

"Yeah!" they all shouted.

"Okay," I said, "let's get to work. Dr. Dread has a new and diabolical scheme up his sleeve. Our job is to spy on his laboratory and see what we can uncover."

"And when we uncover it," the Porcupine growled, "we'll crush it!"

Everyone piled in the Kidmobile. I drove to Dr. Dread's abandoned warehouse on the outskirts of town.

Last time I was there, Dr. Dread had put up an invisible ion force field to keep me out. That hadn't worked, so now the warehouse was surrounded by something a lot more obvious—a twenty-foot-high electric fence.

"What now?" Slime Boy asked.

"No problem," I said. I opened the trunk of the Kidmobile and took out a rope with an anchor attached. Using my superthrowing ability, I flung it onto the roof. It caught on a pipe and held. I attached the other end to the bumper of the Kidmobile.

Quickly, we climbed the rope to the roof. I saw a door.

"I'll go in first and check things out," the Porcupine said. "Back me up."

He opened the door and ran inside. One long minute later, he still hadn't returned. "We can't wait any longer," I cried. "The Porcupine might be in trouble!"

But as we ran toward the door, it flew open. There stood Dr. Dread, surrounded by his army of mutant rats. But something was different. The rats now had robotic arms, telescopic eyeballs, and circuit boards attached to their heads.

"Meet my new friends—the cyborg rats," Dr. Dread said with a cackle.

"Meet my new friends," I said. "The League of SuperDudes."

"What have you done with the Porcupine?" Toolbox demanded.

"Wouldn't you like to know," Dr. Dread sneered. He turned to his rats. "Attack!!"

The battle began. The Blade sliced with his knifelike hands. Slime Boy spit his slime bullets. Toolbox flung poison-tipped nails. I threw exploding baseballs.

But none of it seemed to bother the cyborg rats.

"What now?" the Blade cried.

I looked around. There were old, abandoned warehouses in every direction. "I've got an idea," I shouted. "Follow me!"

I ran to the edge of the roof and jumped. I landed on the next rooftop and rolled to a stop. The rest of the SuperDudes followed. Unfortunately, so did the rats.

We scrambled to our feet and kept running. Every time we came to the edge of a roof, we leaped to the next one. But the rats were still after us—and they were getting closer.

We kept running. Uh-oh! The next building was at least fifty yards away. No way could we jump that far! Then I had an idea. I reached in my backpack and pulled out four aluminum boxes. When I pushed a button on the side of each box, they transformed into four supercharged BMX mini-bikes.

"Hop on," I said. "It's our only chance."

We all climbed on our bikes. Could we make it? The

ground was hundreds of feet below us. If we came up short, it would be all over.

"I'll go first," the Blade said fearlessly. He started pedaling. He hit the edge of the roof and flew out into space. We all held our breath until—yes!—he landed it.

Slime Boy went next. Now it was just Toolbox and me.

"I'm scared," Toolbox said. "What if we don't make it?"

"We'll make it," I said. "Here, give me your hand."

He held out his hand. It was trembling. I took it and held it tight. "Let's do it!" I cried.

We both started pedaling. When we hit the edge of the roof, we flew out into nothingness. One second . . . two seconds . . . then touchdown! We landed on the other roof, lost our balance, and fell off our bikes.

When we got up, our elbows were bleeding. But we were smiling. Then we saw the cyborg rats coming after us. They ran, they jumped . . . they didn't make it! The rooftops echoed with their shrieks as they fell to the ground and splatted like water balloons.

"SuperDudes rule!" a voice cried.

We looked around. It was the Porcupine, and he was standing on the rooftop behind us. "Dr. Dread chained me to the wall of his laboratory," he said.

"But I managed to cut through the chains with my quills and escape."

United again, the SuperDudes walked to the edge of the roof and gazed with satisfaction at the pile of dead rats below.

Toolbox turned to me. "We couldn't have done it without you, Kid," he said. "You've got guts to spare."

October 2

8:13 A.M.

I'm walking across the playground of Yardville Elementary, feeling as self-conscious as a zebra in a pride of lions. I thought my second day as a boy was going to be easier. Instead, I'm so nervous I can hardly put one foot in front of the other.

I keep expecting Ms. Anstine to come running out of the office, shouting, "I checked the records. You're in a lot of trouble, young lady!" Or maybe some boy from my class will nudge his friend and say, "Did she think that haircut was going to fool anyone?" And then he'll run to tell Casey and Zane the terrible truth.

But it doesn't happen. Nobody even looks at me.

They're too busy talking and playing dodgeball and chasing each other around.

At least my clothes—jeans and an orange T-shirt that Stuart outgrew—look okay. Of course, it almost didn't work out that way. Mom insisted I wear a skirt to make up for my supershort haircut. "You don't want your friends mistaking you for a boy, do you?" she asked with something close to horror in her voice.

What could I do? I put on the skirt but slipped the jeans on underneath and rolled up the legs. It looked pretty weird, so I slathered on some lip gloss to distract Mom. Success! She was so busy exclaiming about how pretty my lips looked that she didn't even notice my lumpy legs.

Rob had left early for football practice, so I couldn't bum a ride with him. Besides, I didn't want to take a chance of him overhearing one of my new friends call me John. Instead, I rode my bike. When I reached the end of the block, I circled back to my house. Then I hid in the bushes under the picture window, wiggled out of the skirt, and unrolled my jeans.

Ta-da! Instant boy!

Now the bell is ringing and kids are beginning to make their way into the school. I join the crowd, looking for a familiar face. As I walk inside, a voice calls, "Hey, sonny!"

I keep walking—I'm still not programmed to respond to names like that—until a hand touches my shoulder. I turn around. It's one of the janitors.

"Got a sec?" he asks. "I could use some help with this table."

It's a long wooden table, the kind they have in the library. He's already enlisted an older boy to help him. The kid is standing at one of the corners, waiting.

"Sure," I say. I can't help smiling. Janitors never ask girls to help them move stuff, just like teachers never ask girls to figure out why the overhead projector doesn't work. So if this guy is asking me, I figure I must really look like a boy.

My smile fades a little when we lift the table. It's heavy! We start moving, and I stagger under the weight of it.

"You okay?" the janitor asks.

"Totally," I say, laughing as if I do this sort of thing all the time.

We carry the table for what seems like forever. By the time we finally take it into the library, my biceps are screaming for mercy.

"Thanks, boys," the janitor says as we set it down in the corner. "The librarian will write each of you a late pass."

My arm is shaking as I reach for the pass. But I'm feeling kind of proud too.

As I walk down the hall, I picture the kids in all the classrooms pointing at me and whispering, "Isn't that the macho dude who helped move the library table?"

"Yeah, that's the new kid," someone will answer. "His name is John."

Why, oh why did I drink all that water after recess? Okay, we played hard and I got thirsty. *Really* thirsty. But why didn't I think about what would happen? How could I forget my vow never to go to the bathroom during school hours?

Now our class is lined up, ready to walk to the cafeteria, and I have to go bad. *Can a bladder really explode?* I wonder. *And what happens if it does?*

Oh, man, I have to go!

Zane, Casey, and Spencer turn off into the boys' room. Should I follow them? Let's face it—unless I want to have an accident in my pants, I *have* to follow them!

My stomach is churning as I walk into the lavatory. The first thing I notice is the urinals—three of them lined up against one wall. They look like big porcelain water fountains, but I sure wouldn't want to drink out of them. They smell like a combination of supersweet air freshener and old pee.

The boys head for the urinals, and I dash into a stall. It looks just like a stall in the girls' room, except dirtier. There's toilet paper on the floor and—yuck!—someone forgot to flush. It makes me think of Mom, who's always hassling Rob and Stuart for leaving the bathroom a mess. I thought she was just being prissy, but now I wonder.

I clean off the seat with some toilet paper and sit down. It's quiet—not like the girls' room where everyone is chattering away. And then I realize it's probably bad manners to talk while you're standing at a urinal.

I try to imagine it—standing right next to another guy, peeing. Talk about embarrassing! And what if someone walks into the bathroom and calls your name, and without thinking you turn around and—*blech!* I don't even want to think about it!

Of course, there's probably an up side too. Like it's got to be fast, right? No waiting in long lines for a stall the way girls have to. No wonder my father and brothers finish so fast when they go to the men's room at the movie theater. Meanwhile, Mom and I are standing in line, waiting, waiting, waiting . . .

I hear the urinals flush. "You coming, Frankenstein?" Zane calls.

I flash back to recess. Today Zane picked me to be on his team. He didn't try any rough stuff on me either. I guess that means I've been accepted. It feels good, like I've been chosen to be part of an elite group—sort of the playground version of the marines.

As I leave the stall, I'm thinking about the great touchdown pass I caught at the end of the game. I walk to the sink, not even noticing that Zane, Casey, and Spencer are nudging each other and looking at the ceiling.

And then I do notice, but it's too late because suddenly

something wet and heavy lands on my head. I shriek—
and then freeze. Did I sound like a girl?

If I did, the guys are too busy laughing to notice. In fact,
they're falling all over each other.

I look on the floor. The thing that hit me was a wet
paper towel. We do that in the girls' room, too. You soak
the paper towel in the sink and throw it at the ceiling as
hard as you can. It sticks for a while and then—bombs
away!

Relieved, I allow myself to crack a smile. Then I scoop
up the paper towel and lob it at Zane's head.

12:01 P.M.

We walk through the lunch line and take a seat at one of
the tables. "What's this stuff?" I ask, looking at the lumpy
brown slop on my plate.

"Fried beaver brains," Casey says.

Some girls would be grossed out, I guess, but not me.
"With a side of muskrat guts," I reply, taking a bite. "Mm-
mm, good."

"Hey, Zane, you playing basketball at the Y this year?"
Miguel asks.

"Naw. I've outgrown the Y team. They're still playing
baby ball."

Zane glares at us, like he's daring someone to disagree

with him. But nobody questions him. They just sit there, shoving food into their mouths. Casey lets out a burp, just the way I taught him, and we all laugh.

"Here she comes," Zane says suddenly.

It's the girl who wanted to join our football game. She's walking through the cafeteria, swinging her lunch bag.

"How does she expect to play football with those two balloons on her chest?" Zane smirks. "They've got to slow her down."

At first, I'm baffled. Then I realize what he's talking about. The girl is wearing a bra underneath her blouse. I can see the outline of the straps. This, by itself, is nothing unusual. Lots of fifth-grade girls (not me, of course, but plenty of others) wear bras, whether they need them or not. I guess they think it makes them look more grown-up.

But unlike those girls, this girl really needs it.

"You ever hear of that bird, the blue-footed booby?" Spencer asks. He points to the girl's blue socks. "That's her."

Everyone cracks up, except me.

"Hey, Lucinda," Zane calls. "Nice boobies."

The girl blushes. "Shut up."

Zane looks puzzled. "What? Haven't you ever heard of the blue-footed booby? It's a beautiful bird. Long beak, big chest . . ."

Lucinda looks like she's going to cry. She clutches her lunch bag and hurries away.

I want to tell the guys to leave Lucinda alone. It's not her fault she's growing faster than the rest of the girls. But I'm scared to do anything that might clue the guys in to my secret identity. So instead I distract them by showing off my amazing ability to toss Jell-O cubes high in the air and catch them in my mouth. I learned it from Stuart, back when we both went to Mt. Washington.

"Whoa!" Casey exclaims. "You are a man of many talents, John."

Pretty soon we're all tossing Jell-O cubes in the air, seeing who can catch the most in a row. But I'm still wondering, *Is it true that having breasts slows you down? Because if it is, I don't want them.*

1:55 P.M.

"Is sixty a prime number?" Ms. Anstine asks.

Hailey Dupree's arm is waving in the air. "No," she says before Ms. Anstine can even call on her.

"Okay, let's list the factors."

"Sixty," Ernesto calls. "And one."

Even I know that, and I'm terrible at math.

"Kellie, can you name some others?" Ms. Anstine asks.

Kellie Enderby, resident brainiac, starts listing them all. "Two, three, four . . ."

While Kellie blathers on, I lift the edge of my math

workbook to reveal my SuperKid notebook. I start reading over "Guts to Spare," and pretty soon I'm lost in the story, living the life of a superhero. The League of SuperDudes is at my side, and we're about to ride our BMX mini-bikes off the edge of the roof. I can feel my heart pounding as I take Casey's hand and—

"John Frankenhauser."

I look up, blinking as if I just woke up from a dream. Ms. Anstine is looking at me. Heck, the whole class is looking at me!

"Yes?" I squeak.

"Will you please bring me whatever it is you're hiding under your math book?"

"It's just notes," I stammer. "Math notes."

"Then you won't mind letting me see them," Ms. Anstine says with a smile.

My stomach is grinding like skateboard wheels against a curb. If Ms. Anstine reacts to my stories the way Ms. Pillspring did, I'm in deep doo-doo. She'll call my parents, who will call the school psychologist, who—

No, I realize with a sinking feeling, it's worse than that. If Ms. Anstine calls my parents, she'll find out the truth. John is really Joanie. Then my parents will freak, and the school psychologist will probably recommend locking me up and throwing away the key.

For one brief second, I consider ripping the notebook into little pieces and swallowing them. But that would probably get me into even worse trouble—if it didn't choke me first. Like a prisoner on the way to the electric chair, I walk slowly to Ms. Anstine's desk and hand over the notebook.

3:30 P.M.

"Amigo!" I shout. "Come *on!*"

I'm pedaling to the Yardville Preserve to meet Casey. We're going to start work on the tree house today. But Amigo seems determined to stop and sniff every last leaf, stick, and pile of dirt in the county. Sometimes he just stops for no reason at all. I don't know what's gotten into him.

"Amigo!" I give him a soft whack on the rump. He looks at me and wags his tail. "Hurry up, old man!"

He's not really old. Just five. But today he's acting like he's fifteen.

Finally, we get to the preserve and I take off Amigo's leash. He perks up and goes into pointer mode—head erect, one paw in the air. I follow his nose and see a female deer standing about fifty yards away. The deer is on high alert, frozen, waiting.

Suddenly, Amigo takes off and so does the deer. I'm not worried; the deer has a big head start. Sure enough, she disappears into the trees before Amigo is halfway across the meadow.

I ride down the trail, happy to see my dog acting normal again. It's so beautiful out here, I can almost forget that right at this moment Ms. Anstine might be putting down my SuperKid story, picking up the phone, and—

No, I don't want to think about that now. I stand up on my pedals and soon I'm at the Stiegman Street entrance. Casey is already there, standing beside a wagon filled with scrap wood and tools.

"Want one?" he asks, holding out a cookie.

I grin and take it. It's chocolate chip—my favorite! They're good too. "I wish my mom baked cookies," I said. "Her desserts are usually something weird like crème caramel or hazelnut torte."

"What is she—a chef?" Casey asks.

"No, a home ec. teacher. You know—sewing, cooking, all that."

"My mom should take her course," Casey says. "She can't cook to save her life."

"But—"

"*I* baked the cookies. I do most of the cooking around my house."

"You?" I say, stooping to scratch Amigo as he lopes up beside me. "Why?"

"My parents own a software design company. They're glued to their computers like twelve hours a day."

He looks a little sad and I don't know how to react. What do boys say when their friends are feeling down?

"It's not like they *make* me cook for them," he continues. "They'd be happy to just microwave some soup. But, you know, I kind of like it." He laughs self-consciously. "Is that weird?"

Yes! I want to shout. In my house the only person who cooks is my mom—and me, if she forces me to. But I don't like it. So why does Casey—a boy—think it's fun?

It's all kind of confusing, and I'm not sure what to say. So I go with a joke. "Did you hear about the two kids who got arrested yesterday? One was drinking battery acid, and one was eating fireworks."

A slow grin spreads over Casey's face. "What happened?"

"They charged one and let the other one off."

He bursts out laughing and I join in. "Let's get to work," he says. "I've drawn a sort of plan for how I think this thing should look."

He hands me a piece of paper. "Hey, this is pretty good," I say. "I didn't know you could draw."

He shrugs and takes a bucket and some rope out of the wagon. He throws the rope over a ten-foot-high branch and ties it to the handle of the bucket. Then he fills the bucket with hammers, nails, and pieces of wood.

"I'll climb up, and you can send the wood up to me," he says. "Then you follow me."

Wow, I think, *Casey is really clever.* I would have tried to climb the tree and carry the stuff at the same time. I'm even more impressed when we get up there. Casey fits a board in the crook of the tree and nails it down like an experienced carpenter.

I grab the second hammer and try to imitate Casey. But all I manage to do is bend the nail.

"Didn't your dad ever teach you to use a hammer?" he asks.

"I've never seen my dad use a tool in my entire life," I answer honestly. "Unless you count a stethoscope."

"He's a doctor?"

I nod. "My mother's the one who's good with her hands. She can sew, knit, crochet. Once she embroidered a tablecloth with a map of the world on it."

"My parents aren't exactly handy," Casey explains. "They can change a lightbulb; that's about it. My grandfather taught me how to use tools."

After a few instructions, I manage to get a nail through a board without destroying the nail *or* my finger. Pretty cool!

"How do you like Yardville so far?" Casey asks as we work.

So far. I try to picture the year ahead. Until this moment, I haven't really thought about the future. I mean, how long can I keep up this boy act? And what happens if I don't?

"It's okay, I guess," I reply. "It's hard having to make all new friends."

Casey shoots me a shy smile. "You've got one already."

I look into his eyes, and my heart does a funny little rabbit hop. He looks at me quizzically. Does he know the truth? My stomach tightens.

"Tell me about the Y basketball league," I say, looking away. "It's all boys, right?"

"It was. They're going co-ed this year."

"Is that why Zane isn't joining?" I ask.

"Probably. Zane plays to win, and he doesn't like anything—or anyone—to slow him down."

"If he plays b-ball like he plays football, watch out," I say.

Casey nods. "Zane's the strongest, the fastest, the toughest—"

I think about what Zane said to Lucinda at lunch today. "The meanest," I add.

Casey considers. "He can be that too. I guess it's just part of the package."

So is that how it works when you're a boy? I wonder. *The tougher and meaner you are, the more your friends look up to you?* I pick up a nail and hold it in place. Then I lift my hammer and focus all the rough, tough-boy energy I can muster on its tiny steel head.

Whap! I miss the nail and put a crack in the board.

Casey laughs and shakes his head. I guess I've still got a lot to learn.

"Amigo, hurry up! We're going to be late."

Amigo looks at me like he doesn't understand what I'm saying. It's so unlike him. Usually he runs right beside my bike—or even runs ahead, pulling me off balance. But today he's dragging like an anchor in quicksand.

I give his leash a tug. Mom hates it if we're late for dinner. It's like a performance for her—Priscilla Frankenhauser and Her Amazing Food. You have to be in your seat and ready to chew or she goes ballistic.

Dad is big on the whole family dinner thing too but for a different reason. He says it's the only time he ever sees all of us in the same place at the same time.

Finally, Amigo slows to a walk and won't speed up no matter how hard I pull on him. Now I'm getting worried. I get off my bike and walk it the rest of the way. Amigo plods along beside me. When I reach down to scratch his rump, he pulls away.

"Dad!" I call, flinging open the front door. "Dad, come quick!"

It's Mom who appears first. "What's wrong?"

"I think Amigo's hurt."

Dad walks down the stairs, drying his hands. He tosses the towel on the bannister, and the three of us go outside. Amigo is lying in the grass beside my bike. Dad kneels down and examines him, starting at his head and working his way down Amigo's body. When he touches Amigo's furry stomach, my dog lets out a yelp.

"What is it?" I ask.

Dad ignores me. "It's okay, boy," he says, gently pressing Amigo's belly. Amigo winces but doesn't pull away.

Dad clears his throat. "There's a mass here," he says, glancing up at Mom and me. "A hard spot."

"What does it mean?" I ask anxiously.

"I'm not a vet. I suggest we take him into the pet clinic tomorrow."

"Dad, come on!" I whine. "You must have some idea."

He stands up and puts his arm around my shoulders. "There's no point in guessing, Joanie. It could be something. It could be nothing much at all. An X-ray will give us more information."

I turn to Mom.

"I'll call the vet first thing tomorrow," she says, squeezing my shoulders. "Now let's go in. Dinner is ready."

"But what about Amigo? We can't leave him out here."

Dad picks him up and carries him into the garage. Amigo doesn't even struggle. Dad lowers him onto his dog bed.

"I'll make him a plate of leftovers," Mom says as we walk inside. "You know how much he loves my pork chops."

I love them too. But when I sit down to dinner, I can barely eat a bite. I'm too worried about Amigo. Up until today, he's run on two speeds—overdrive and off. Slow just wasn't an option. But now . . .

I think about what Dad said. "It could be something. It could be nothing much at all."

I've got a bad feeling it's something.

I'm in the restroom at the mini-mart, hurriedly changing into my shorts. My heart is pounding like a pile driver because I almost ran right into Zane! He was coming out of the mini-mart as I was getting off my bike. I had to dart behind a pickup truck so he wouldn't see me.

I shudder, imagining what would have happened if he'd spotted me in a skirt. The thought is so horrible, my mind won't even go there. Instead, I take the sick feeling inside me and turn it into an angry one. It isn't hard. All I have to do is remember what happened this morning.

I was climbing on my bike, ready to ride to school. Amigo was there beside me, wagging his tail and looking ready for action. Probably the lump Dad felt last night was just an undigested mouse.

Suddenly, I heard Mom's voice behind me. "Joanie!"

It wasn't a friendly "Joanie" or an alarmed "Joanie." It was a you're-about-to-catch-it "Joanie."

My stomach tightened as I turned around. She was standing in the bushes, holding the crumpled skirt from yesterday morning. Oops. I'd meant to throw that in the laundry.

"What is this doing here?" she asked in her best school-teacher voice.

"I must have dropped it."

"You must have taken it off. What were you wearing under it?"

"Jeans," I admitted.

"I don't understand you, Joanie. Are you *trying* to look unattractive?"

The words felt like cold water on my skin. I blurted out the first thing that came into my head. "So I guess I should hide my face under a pound of makeup like you do."

"What you should do is care about your appearance," she snapped. "Now march in there and put on this skirt."

"But it's probably got ants in it!"

"I don't care. Get in there—*now!*"

I did as she told me. When I came out, she looked me over. "At least now no one will mistake you for a boy."

That's what I was afraid of. Fortunately, I'd managed to shove my shorts into my backpack.

Now, as I slip them on, her parting words pop into my head. "What happened to that pink sweater I lent you on the first day of school?"

Good question. I make a mental note to look in the Lost and Found at recess.

Before I leave the restroom, I glance in the mirror. *Do I really look unattractive? My new friends—Zane, Casey, the rest of the guys—don't think so, do they?* The thought that they might leaves a strange empty feeling in the middle of my chest.

But then I remind myself, I'm just one of the guys to them. They probably wouldn't pay any attention to my looks unless there was something really unusual about me—one blue eye and one brown, something like that.

That should make me feel better but it doesn't. All I feel is confused.

The feeling ends fast when I walk out of the restroom and look at the clock on the mini-mart wall. Eight-fifteen! Uh-oh! I'm late for school!

10:45 A.M.

Things are looking up! Ms. Anstine didn't punish me for being late, and so far she hasn't mentioned my SuperKid stories. Maybe she forgot all about it.

The bell rings for recess and Zane jumps up, imitating

73

the announcer on the NFL commercials. "Are you ready for some football?"

"You know it," I reply as we head for the door.

"John," Ms. Anstine calls, "may I speak with you a minute?"

Oh, no! My optimism sinks like the *Titanic*. I glance at Zane. He rolls his eyes and says, "Later, dude."

My stomach does a backflip as I take a seat next to Ms. Anstine's desk. I just know I'm in trouble. Big, big trouble.

She prolongs the agony by waiting until every last kid leaves the room.

Empire State Building trouble, I think as my palms grow damp. *Grand Canyon trouble*.

My notebook is lying on her desk. She taps it and says, "You're a very good writer, John."

"Thank you," I mumble. I know she's just trying to lull me into a false sense of security before she tightens the noose.

"Excellent storytelling," she continues, leafing through the pages. "Very fast-paced and exciting. And I like the way you deal with themes of bravery and loyalty."

I let myself relax a little. *Why was I so worried?* I wonder. Ms. Anstine thinks I'm a boy, and boys are allowed to write stories like mine. The only problem is I'm not a boy. I ask myself what Ms. Anstine would think if she knew the truth. The answer isn't pretty.

"Your stories are very raw, very violent," she says.

I tense. Here it comes. But to my amazement, she doesn't look upset. Just thoughtful. Still, I feel the urge to apologize—or at least explain.

"It's just pretend," I tell her. "I don't do stuff like that in real life."

She lets out a little chuckle. "I didn't think you did."

Then she cocks her head and looks at me. It's like she's studying me, trying to decide something. At first I look back. She's got nice blue eyes, bright and twinkly like the sun on the ocean. But five seconds later, she's still looking at me, and it's starting to feel weird. My eyes dart nervously around the room.

"Sometimes people use art as a way to express the intense emotions they feel inside," she says at last. "Emotions like anger and frustration."

She looks like she expects a response, so I nod.

"It's a good way to deal with your feelings," she continues. "A healthy way. Much better than taking them out on the people around you." She pauses. "Much better than keeping secrets."

Secrets? Suddenly, I can't breathe. She knows the truth. Oh, no, I'm about to be busted!

But Ms. Anstine just smiles and hands me my notebook. "Go out to recess, John."

I grab the notebook and jump up like a jack-in-the-box. Tossing it on my desk, I walk toward the door.

"John?" she calls.

I turn around. "Yeah?"

"Keep writing. You've got talent."

I feel a grin stealing up my cheeks. "Thanks!"

Walking down the hall, I think about what Ms. Anstine said about using art as a way to express intense emotions.

What does that have to do with me? I wonder. *I'm not angry or frustrated.*

Well, except sometimes. Like this morning when Mom made me wear that stupid skirt. Or back at Mount Washington when Randy Soworski wouldn't throw me the football. And when Mrs. Pillspring told my parents about my SuperKid story—that was the worst!

But here at Yardville Elementary, everything is different. Now I'm John, and I don't have any of those problems.

I throw open the door and walk out onto the playground. Casey looks up from the huddle and motions me over. I break into a run, my heart lifting. I was right to think things are looking up. Ms. Anstine isn't going to get on my case about my SuperKid stories. And my new friends—my *guy* friends—have accepted me completely.

If that isn't Easy Street, I don't know what is.

12:12 P.M.

"Why'd Ms. Anstine keep you in at recess?" Spencer asks between bites of his peanut butter and jelly sandwich.

"It was about that notebook she took from you yesterday, wasn't it?" Zane says.

Every time I talk about my SuperKid stories, things get complicated. So I just shrug instead.

The guys pick up on my silence instantly. "What was it?" Ernesto asks. "A note to a girl?"

"No way!" I cry. I don't have to lie about that!

"A cartoon of Ms. Anstine?" Casey suggests.

I shake my head and stick my straw into my juice box.

"Come on, out with it," Zane says.

"It's stories, that's all," I mumble.

"What kind of stories?" Casey asks. He looks so sincerely interested, I'm almost ready to tell him.

"Let's see them," Zane says before I can answer.

"Huh?"

"I said, let's see them. Right here, right now. Hand 'em over."

"Forget it," I say, looking away.

"Hey, I thought you were our friend," Zane presses. "Friends share. Right, guys?"

"Right," they all agree.

They've got their eyes trained on me like rifle barrels, waiting to see what I'm going to do. Nobody says anything, but I get the feeling that if I don't turn over the stories, I'm going to pay. No more football games at recess. No friends to eat lunch with. In fact, no friends, period.

Zane clears his throat and holds out his hand, palm up. It's now or never.

I'm about to do it when I remember something absolutely catastrophic. Some of my stories say *Joanie* on them. My brain goes into overdrive, and I come up with a makeshift plan to give myself time to replace *Joanie* with *John*.

"I'll show them to you, but not until the end of recess," I blurt out.

"Aw, come on! Why?" the guys ask.

"I have to get everything just right. Now get out of here, and don't come back until five minutes before the bell rings."

Zane gives me a disgusted look, but I throw it right back at him. With a snort, he and the boys walk away.

Thirty minutes later, the guys are there, staring at me impatiently. Reluctantly, I reach in my backpack and pull out my notebook. Zane grabs it and flips to the first page— my first SuperKid story. Everybody leans in, reading over his shoulder. My insides are rocking like a tugboat in a typhoon. Will they like it? Or will they think it's lame?

The seconds tick by. Zane turns the page. Then, finally, he looks up. "I didn't know you could write, Frankenstein."

"It's good!" Casey declares.

"Yeah, pretty cool," Spencer says.

The other kids nod their agreement. I'm grinning like an idiot. They like it!

"I bet Casey could do some killer illustrations," Ernesto suggests.

"Sure," Casey agrees. He turns to me. "I mean, if you wanted me to."

"That would be awesome!" I cry, completely forgetting to act cool.

"When I'm finished, I could run it through my parents' scanner," he continues. "We could turn it into a book."

"And charge everyone in the school a quarter to read it," Zane adds with a smirk.

The bell rings, and we scarf down the last of our food. I reach for the notebook, but Zane stops me. "Can I borrow it for the rest of the afternoon? I want to keep reading."

I should say no. What if Ms. Anstine catches him looking at it during class? I doubt she'll be so understanding the second time around. But I'm just so stoked he likes my stories.

"Sure," I reply.

2:30 P.M.

When school ends, Zane is waiting for me outside the classroom. He hands me the notebook.

"Thanks," I say and turn to go.

"Hang on. I want to talk to all the guys."

All the guys! I still can't believe that includes me. We stand around, waiting for Casey, Ernesto, Spencer, and Miguel to appear. When they do, Zane gathers us around him.

"I think we should start a real League of SuperDudes," he says. "All of you can be in it—if you qualify."

"What do you mean?" Casey asks. "Do we have to take a bath in radioactive waste or something?"

Everybody snickers, but Zane just rolls his eyes. "Okay, so we don't have real superpowers. Big deal. We're still the toughest, bravest dudes around. To prove it, I'm going to think up three tests. If you pass them, you're in the gang."

"Why you?" Spencer asks.

Zane steps up to him, so close their noses are almost touching. "Because I'm the baddest dude in this school, and I can beat your butt. You want me to show you?"

It only takes a second for Spencer to turn away. "Okay, okay," he mutters. "What's the first test?"

Zane doesn't hesitate. Apparently, he's been thinking this over. "You know that tree in the Yardville Preserve—the one on the edge of the cliff?"

"The one you climbed?" Casey asks.

Zane nods. "That's the first test. You've got to climb that tree and hang out over the edge of the cliff by your knees."

I think about the day Casey showed me that tree. I couldn't believe anyone would climb it, let alone hang from the branch. Then I try to picture myself climbing it. Fear flows through me like electricity. I glance around the circle. The boys are scared too.

"It's too dangerous," Casey pipes up. "If you fell from that tree, you'd break your neck."

"Then you'd better not fall," Zane replies.

"Come on, man," Ernesto says, trying to laugh. "Not all of us have a death wish like you."

"Do it," Zane says evenly, "or you can't be in the League of SuperDudes."

There's a second of silence while we all consider this. Then Zane says, "I'm heading over there right now. Who's got the guts to join me?"

He doesn't wait for an answer. He just turns around and starts walking. The rest of us glance uneasily at each other, wondering what to do. Then Spencer runs to catch up with Zane. Ernesto and Miguel are the next to commit.

Now it's just Casey and me. I try to catch his eye, but he's staring at his shoes. Then, slowly, head still lowered, he shuffles after Zane and the guys.

I stand there, wondering what to do. I'm scared—so scared my knees are weak. Still, I don't want to get left behind. This is the first time I've ever been part of a group. The first time I've ever been accepted. I don't want to blow it now. Besides, how hard can it be to climb that stupid tree?

I'm about to find out.

It turns out everyone except Ernesto rode bikes to school. Spencer's bike has trick pedals, so Ernesto stands on the back, and we all head over to the preserve. Nobody talks on the way there. I guess we're all too busy thinking about what's coming.

When the big twisted oak tree comes into view, I feel my stomach turn over. The tree is even less stable than I remembered. Big roots are sticking out of the side of the cliff, dangling into nothingness. And that branch—it doesn't look strong enough to hold Amigo, let alone a kid.

Zane throws down his bike and strides over to the tree. He climbs it like a spider, and soon he's shinnying out over the ravine. I watch with awe as he wraps his legs around the branch and hangs from it. He shoots us an upside-down grin and clasps his hands together like a prizefighter who just scored a knockout.

"Piece of cake," he declares as he saunters back to join us. "Who's next?"

We all look at each other. Then Spencer says, "I'll go."

He's not as fast or as confident as Zane, but he makes it out onto the branch. He locks his knees and leans back, hands still clutching the branch. Then slowly he releases his grip and lets his arms fall free. One second . . . two . . . He grasps the branch and sits up. He did it!

Ernesto volunteers next. As he shinnies across the branch, a big clump of dirt falls from the exposed roots and tumbles down the cliff into the ravine. Ernesto hesitates. "You sure this is safe?" he calls.

"No," Zane calls back. "That's the point, isn't it?"

Ernesto sets his jaw and hangs from the branch. Then he's down so fast he's almost a blur.

Casey and I glance nervously at each other. Who's next?

"Go on, Casey," Zane says.

I watch with relief as Casey walks to the tree. He looks a little unsteady on his feet. When he climbs, he slips twice and almost falls.

Finally, he reaches the branch. He hangs on tight, chin almost touching the bark, and inches out over the ravine. The tree creaks softly. Casey freezes, his eyes wide with fear.

"Do it!" Zane calls. "Hurry up!"

Casey is lying, stomach down, on the branch. He's got his legs wrapped around it so tightly, I worry it's going to snap off. Now he leans gingerly over the edge of the branch and lets his arms hang down. He's not hanging by his knees—not the way Zane did. But before anyone can protest, he scoots back to the tree and starts climbing down.

Zane shakes his head. "What was *that*, Dilliplane?"

"The branch was creaking, man," Casey answers. "I thought it was going to crack."

Crack? My chest tightens. Is he serious?

"Is he in?" Spencer asks impatiently.

Zane considers. "I'll give you a break this time, Dilliplane," he says. "But next test, you'd better go all out."

Casey nods and turns away. He looks like he wants to rake up some leaves and crawl under them.

Then suddenly, Miguel pipes up, "I—I gotta go."

Everyone turns to stare at him.

"Yeah," he says nervously, "I forgot. I'm supposed to be at a dentist appointment right now. My mother'll kill me if I don't show up."

"Get serious, dude," Zane scoffs. "You don't have a dentist appointment. You're just chicken."

Miguel looks like a cornered rabbit. "Look, what's the big deal? I could climb that tree with my eyes closed."

"Then why don't you do it?" Spencer demands.

"'Cause it's stupid!" Miguel turns and picks up his bike. "I'm outta here."

"Wuss!" Zane calls as Miguel rides away. "Loser!"

"So long, wimp!" Ernesto shouts.

Spencer picks up a rock and throws it. It sails over Miguel's head.

"No guts, no glory!" Zane calls after him.

Miguel disappears around a stand of trees, pedaling furiously. Right then and there, I decide I'm not going to wimp out. I run to the tree and scramble up it like there's a bear on my tail. When I reach the branch, I crawl out to the middle before I have a chance to think about it. Then I stop and make the mistake of looking down. Oh, man! The little creek in the ravine looks miles away. And those exposed roots—they're like angry pythons just waiting to grab me when I fall.

"What are you waiting for?" Zane calls.

I think the other guys are calling encouragement—or maybe insults. Blood is pumping in my ears so hard that I can't hear. I scoot sideways and wrap my legs around the branch. The tree lets out a low groan. It sounds like it can't take it anymore, like it's about to give up the ghost. Chunks of loose soil tumble down the cliff. I hear a distant *plop, plop, plop* as they hit the creek.

Panic is rising in my chest, pushing against my breastbone like a monster trying get out. *Do it*, I tell myself. *Do it now!*

I take my hands off the branch and lean back. *Whoa!* I'm hanging by my knees! I don't know what it looks like because my eyes are squeezed shut, but I'm definitely doing it.

The sounds of the guys applauding and whistling set me in motion again. I have to get off this tree before it falls down the cliff!

The next thing I remember, I'm standing on the ground and Zane is punching me in the arm. "You're in," he says.

Suddenly, all my fear is gone. I feel like throwing my arms in the air and doing a crazy touchdown dance. This boy thing is a snap. A walk in the park. And oh, man, it feels so good!

All the guys gather around Zane. He thrusts his arm into the center of the circle and makes a fist. We lay our hands on his, just like in a football huddle. "SuperDudes rule!" he shouts.

"SuperDudes rule!" we bellow back.

Our voices reverberate through the trees, making them tremble. And that stupid oak tree—if Zane snapped his fingers, it would bow down at our feet.

6:30 P.M.

Here with the guys, I know where I stand. I'm accepted; I fit in. It feels good. But if I don't get home by dinnertime, I'll catch it.

As I pedal toward my house, my pumped-up ego slowly deflates. Soon I'll be sitting at the dinner table, hearing

86

Mom's critical comments on my hair, my posture, my clothes. . . .

Oh, no! I left the house in a skirt. If I come home in shorts, Mom will freak. I dump my bike in the driveway and slip into the bushes. I'm pulling my skirt out of my backpack when Mom opens the front door.

"Joanie, where are you?"

I crouch down and wait, not moving, not even breathing.

"*Joan*-ie!" she calls. "Family meeting! Now!"

Uh-oh. I just hope this doesn't have anything to do with me. I wiggle out of my shorts and pull on my skirt. Then I hurry inside.

Amigo meets me in the hallway, tail wagging. But he's limping a little, and he doesn't jump on me the way he usually does. I lean over to pet him and he licks my hand.

"Joanie, is that you?" Mom calls.

I follow her voice into the dining room. Everyone is sitting around the table, but there's no food in sight. "Hey," I say, slipping into my seat.

Rob and Stuart nod at me. Mom pats my hand while Dad clears his throat. Man, this is serious. My body tenses like when I'm about to get a shot.

"I took Amigo to the pet clinic today," Mom says. "They examined him and took some X-rays."

"And?" Rob asks impatiently.

"Dr. McCullough called me this afternoon," Dad says. "Amigo has a tumor on his large intestine."

"You mean cancer?" I ask in disbelief.

Dad nods. "She can operate, but there's only a fifty-fifty chance she can get it all. Even if she does, there's no guarantee it hasn't spread to his stomach lining or even his lymph system."

"So what are you saying?" Stuart asks, his forehead wrinkling beneath his stringy hair. "Is Amigo going to die?"

"My honest opinion?" Dad answers. "Yes. If Dr. McCullough operates, it might not be right away. If we put Amigo down . . ."

"Put him to sleep?" I gasp.

"It's an option. Probably the most humane one."

"No!" I cry.

"Joanie, we can't explain to Amigo what's going on," Dad says. "If Dr. McCullough does the surgery, all Amigo will know is that he's in a cage, away from his familiar surroundings, and he hurts. I don't think he should have to go through that, especially since we can't promise he's not going to relapse."

"But he *might* get better," I insist, "right?"

"He might. But remember, he isn't going to bounce back immediately. He'll have to wear one of those plastic funnel-shaped collars so he doesn't chew his stitches. He won't be able to go outside, and that means we'll have to clean up after him. It isn't going to be pretty." He turns to Mom. "It isn't going to be cheap either."

I look under the table. Amigo sticks his head between my knees and eyes me quizzically. I try to picture him with stitches on his belly and a plastic funnel around his neck. It doesn't seem possible.

"Maybe you're right," Rob says, frowning like Dad does when he's making a diagnosis. "Maybe it would be better to put Amigo out of his misery."

"He's not miserable!" I protest.

"Not yet," Dad says.

The words send a shiver down the back of my neck. I push the feeling aside. Amigo's going to get better. He just has to.

"All I know is I'm not cleaning up any dog poop," Stuart declares, wrinkling his nose.

"Remember that the next time Stuart gets a stomach virus," I tell Mom. "If he barfs, make him clean it up himself."

"Let's not fight," Dad breaks in. "Joanie, I assume you're voting for the surgery. Rob, Stu, you're against it, right?"

Rob nods his head. "I think what you said makes sense, Dad."

Stuart shrugs. "Whatever. He's Joanie's dog, right? Shouldn't she decide?"

"I want to hear everyone's opinion," Dad replies. "Then your mom and I will do what we think is best."

Everyone turns to Mom. She hasn't said a word through all of this. What's she thinking? I can't exactly see *her* cleaning up Amigo's poop. She doesn't even like vacuuming up his hair.

Mom folds her hands on the table. "If I were in Amigo's position," she says softly, "I wouldn't give up—even if I only had a million-to-one chance." She looks around the table. "If Amigo could understand what's going on, I don't think he'd want to give up either."

"Priscilla," Dad asks, "what are you saying?"

"I think he should have the surgery."

I can't believe it! Mom is on Amigo's side—on *my* side!

"It's going to be a lot of work," Dad says. "And a big expense."

"You said that already," I mutter.

"Joanie, I'm not trying to be cruel. Just the opposite. I'm trying to save Amigo from a slow, painful death."

"Whatever happens, I'll take care of him," Mom says. She glances at me. "*We'll* take care of him."

We? My mother and I can't set the table together without getting into a fight. How are we going to deal with a sick dog?

I don't know the answer. But if it means saving Amigo's life, I'll definitely give it a try.

October 4

10:45 A.M.

It's my fourth day as a boy, and I'm getting used to it. I hardly ever have to remind myself to slouch or burp or keep my voice low and even. It's all pretty much second nature now.

Today I'm too preoccupied to worry much about it anyway. I'm worrying about Amigo instead. He had his surgery this morning at ten o'clock. I wanted to stay home, so I could go to the vet with Mom, but she said no. I reminded her that she could use all the help she could get. The last time we took Amigo to Dr. McCullough's, Amigo chased a yippy little Chihuahua into the street and almost caused a traffic accident. But she still wouldn't give in.

I try to lose myself in our recess basketball game. It's not my best sport. I haven't made a basket since we started, but I've tried to make up for it by showing off my defensive skills. I've managed to steal the ball three times already.

Now Zane goes up for a basket. He's just as good at basketball as he is at football. Better even, because he's taller than all the rest of us. *Swoosh!* Nothing but net.

As Casey takes the ball out of bounds, I notice Lucinda leaning up against the corner of the school, watching us. It's easy to read her mind. She's got the same look of longing on her face that I used to wear back at Mt. Washington.

Man, I feel for her. Once I was on the outside, desperate to get in. Now I'm tight with Zane and his crew, but only because they think I'm one of them. If they knew the truth, I'd be standing there with Lucinda.

The bell rings. Zane drops the ball, and the guys head back to class. I veer off and walk toward Lucinda. I meet up with her at the tetherball pole. "Hi," I say. "You're Lucinda, right?"

She eyes me warily. She knows I'm part of Zane's gang.

"Do you play basketball at the Y?" I ask.

She nods. "Why?"

"No reason. I just wondered. I mean, I know you're good at sports." When she doesn't answer, I say, "My name's—"

A voice behind me cuts me off. "Look who's got the hots for Lucinda!"

I spin around and there's Zane, grinning at me. Spencer, Ernesto, and Casey are standing behind him.

"Shut up," I mumble.

"She's got something John wants," Spencer says suggestively.

Ernesto snorts a laugh. "Yeah, Lucinda, why don't you go into the bushes and show it—I mean, *them*."

I look over at Lucinda. She's blushing beet red. I want to say something to defend her, but how can I? Zane and the guys expect me to join in their dissing. If I don't, I'll never live it down.

Fortunately, I'm saved by the arrival of Hailey Dupree and Miranda Bennett. "Why don't you leave her alone?" Hailey demands, hands on hips.

"Yeah, pick on someone your own brain size," Miranda says. "You know, subhuman."

Zane snickers. "You two are just jealous because you're both flat as a chalkboard."

It's not really true. Both girls wear bras—I've seen the outline under their blouses. Miranda even has a little something to put in hers. In fact, if there's a girl in this group who's flat as a chalkboard, it's me.

I'm not sure what to think about that. If Zane and the guys knew I was a girl, they'd completely ignore me. But if

I was built like Lucinda—forget it! I don't want that kind of attention.

The playground monitor claps her hands. "Girls and boys, back to class!"

"Come on, Lucinda," Hailey says. She and Miranda link arms with Lucinda, and they strut across the blacktop together.

Zane laughs. "There they go—the blue-footed booby and the String Bean Sisters."

The boys keep up the jokes as we stroll back to class. I look away. This whole boy-girl thing is so confusing I don't know what to think. The only one who isn't saying anything is Casey.

I glance over at him. His face is blank, totally impassive. I wonder what he's thinking.

2:30 P.M.

When school ends, Zane calls us all together. "I think you guys are ready for test number two," he says.

Spencer sticks out his chest a little. Ever since he hung from the oak tree, he's been acting a little more confident, a little more outspoken. He's been tighter with Zane too. "What is it?" he asks.

"You know that old guy who lives at the end of the street? The one who's always yelling at us?"

I know who he means. There's a white-haired man who lives in the last house before the corner. After school, he stands at his picture window, just waiting for some kid to throw a candy wrapper on the sidewalk or accidentally step on his lawn. Then he's out on the porch in a flash, screaming that kids have no respect these days, and we'd better get lost or he'll call the cops.

"His name's Mr. Corolla," Ernesto says. "He goes to my church."

"He's a pain," Zane says, "and I think it's about time we did something about it."

"Like what?" Casey asks.

"Meet me at the flagpole right after dark," he replies. "We're going to show Old Man Corolla he can't mess around with the League of SuperDudes."

What does he have in mind? I hope it's not as dangerous as our last challenge. "Zane," I begin. "I—"

"Be here or you can forget about being in the Super-Dudes," he says, cutting me off. Then he walks to the bike stand and starts unlocking his bike.

Spencer and Ernesto hurry after him.

"You want to work on the tree house this afternoon?" Casey asks me.

"I can't. My dog had an operation this morning. I have to go home and find out how he's doing."

"That stinks. What's wrong with him?"

"Cancer. But . . . but he's going to be all right." I want to believe it, but I'm not so sure. What if Dad's right? What if Amigo is going to die?

Casey watches as Zane, Spencer, and Ernesto ride away. Then he says, "What do think Zane has in mind for tonight?"

"I was wondering that myself."

Casey looks away. "I barely passed the last test. I can't wimp out this time."

"But what if . . . ?" My voice trails off. "What if it's something really bad?"

"Then we don't have to do it, right?"

I'm not sure if he's telling me or asking me. I think it over. Of course we don't *have* to do what Zane says. But if we don't, we won't be the toughest, bravest boys in the school, will we? We won't be SuperDudes.

"I'll see you tonight," I say.

Casey nods. "Later."

4:14 P.M.

I hear the front door open and I leap off my bed. "Mom?" I call, running to the landing. "Mom, how is he?"

"The surgery went well," she says, climbing the stairs. "I just spoke to Dr. McCullough. Amigo's resting. If he's doing okay tomorrow, we can bring him home."

"Did they cut out all the cancer?"

"Dr. McCullough thinks so. Only time will tell."

I let out a triumphant whoop and slide down the banister.

"Joanie, please. You sound like a wild animal." Mom walks up to me and pulls the little pixie curls from behind my ears. "There, that looks better. Now take the chicken out of the refrigerator and wash it. I'll be down in a minute to start dinner."

I let out a groan. How can Casey enjoy cooking? I hate it!

I shuffle to the kitchen and toss the package of chicken into the sink. Then I grab a soda and a slice of the pear tart Mom baked yesterday. It's so weird not to see Amigo at my feet, begging for crumbs. I wonder how he's feeling right now. Pretty out of it, I bet. I just hope he isn't hurting.

I'm washing the slimy, disgusting chicken when Mom walks in. "What are you going to make?" I ask.

"Tomatoes stuffed with curried chicken."

I wrinkle my nose. "Why can't you make plain old fried chicken once in a while? Or better yet, we could go to KFC."

Now it's Mom's nose that's wrinkling. "Deep-fried foods are bad for you." She takes a knife from the drawer and begins cutting the chicken.

I watch her chop-chop-chopping. My mother is such a straight arrow. Doesn't she ever feel like just kicking off her shoes and stuffing a couple of Twinkies in her mouth?

I try to imagine her when she was my age. I've seen the

photos. She wore pigtails and cute little dresses, and she always had a sweet smile on her face. I sigh as I toss the last piece of chicken onto the cutting board. I'll bet she never did anything wild or naughty or dangerous. I bet I would have hated her.

The back door opens, and Rob and Stuart burst in.

"Sara Cole is coming over to study with me," Rob announces. "Let me know when she gets here." He grabs the last of the pear tart—pan and all—and heads upstairs.

"Hey," Stuart shouts, running after him, "save some for me!" I hear them struggling and laughing on the stairs.

Neither one of them so much as mentioned Amigo. Do they even care if he lives or dies? Does anybody in this family care except me?

Mom removes a piece of fatty, forbidden chicken skin from one of the breasts. She looks down at the floor, where Amigo would normally be nudging our legs. "What am I going to do with all these scraps?" she asks.

Is it just my imagination, or does she look a little sad as she drops them into the garbage?

8:00 P.M.

I'm standing under the flagpole, waiting for the guys to show up. I told my parents I was going to the preserve. I told them I'd be home before dark. What will I tell them when I get home?

I'm thinking it over when Zane, Spencer, and Ernesto pedal up. Casey shows up a few minutes later. "Okay, we're all here," Zane says. He reaches in his pocket, grinning with anticipation. "Check this out."

We all lean in to see what he's got in his hand. Firecrackers—two or three dozen of them!

"Aren't those illegal?" Casey asks.

"Not in Mississippi," Zane replies. "My cousin gave them to me last Fourth of July."

"What's the plan?" Ernesto asks.

"Simple. We toss them into Old Man Corolla's backyard and watch him go nuts."

Everyone laughs, except me. All I manage is a weak "huh." I'm thinking about what will happen if Mr. Corolla calls the cops.

"Let's move out," Zane says.

We all hop on our bikes and pedal up the street to Mr. Corolla's house. There's a light on in the living room. Zane gets off his bike and wheels it around to the back of the house. We do the same.

Mr. Corolla's backyard has a tall wooden fence around it. Behind the fence is a patch of grass with some bushes and a couple of trees, and beyond that is the parking lot of a medical building. Zane drops his bike in the grass, and we follow him. Standing on tiptoe, we can just see over the fence. By the glow of the porch light, we make out a picnic bench, an old push lawn mower, and a cracked birdbath.

"Ready to rumble?" Zane asks with a thin smile. He takes out the firecrackers and a book of matches.

"What if we set his backyard on fire?" Spencer asks with a nervous laugh.

"Not gonna happen," Zane says. He lights a match and holds it to the end of one of the firecrackers. We all jump back as the flame catches. Zane cracks up. "Come on, you big babies. It's a firecracker, not a hand grenade."

He tosses it over the fence. It explodes with a sharp crack.

"Who's next?" he asks. "Come on, Spence. You didn't back down from the last challenge."

Spencer seems to grow taller under Zane's approving gaze. He lights a firecracker and throws it over the fence. "Bombs away!" he cries.

Crack!

"What about you, Ernesto?" Zane asks. "Spencer outdid you on the last challenge. You don't want him to show you up again, do you, man?"

Ernesto scowls and grabs a string of firecrackers out of Zane's hands. He lights them all and hurls them into the darkness. The sound is like machine-gun fire.

Suddenly, we hear a door fly open. "Who's out there?

What's going on?" It's Mr. Corolla, and he sounds mad and scared.

Zane snickers as he lights two more firecrackers and flings them over the fence.

Pop! Pop!

I peek through a crack in the fence. Mr. Corolla is running across the lawn in his pajamas.

"He's coming this way!" I hiss.

We all run behind the bushes and crouch there, waiting. I glance at Casey. He looks as freaked out as I feel.

"Who's out there?" Mr. Corolla shouts. "Show your face!"

Nobody moves; nobody speaks. We're like four frightened rabbits, trying to blend in with our surroundings.

"I think they're gone, Murphy," Mr. Corolla says at last. "Are you coming inside?"

Spencer mouths the words, "Who's Murphy?"

Zane shrugs. "I've got one more string of firecrackers," he whispers. "Throw it quick, Casey, before he goes inside."

"Me?" Casey gulps.

Zane shakes his head. "Man, after the way you screwed up the other day, I figured you'd be dying to prove yourself."

"Guess not," Ernesto scoffs.

Spencer makes a face. "What a loser!"

"Don't call me that," Casey snaps.

"Well, you're no SuperDude, I'll tell you that," says Zane.

Casey presses his lips together. *Is he going to cry?* I wonder. Suddenly, he snatches the firecrackers out of Zane's hands and runs to the fence. With trembling hands, he lights them and lobs them into the backyard.

Pop! Pop! Pop! Pop!

Suddenly, a high-pitched screech splits the night. We all freeze, eyes wide with fear.

"Murphy!" Mr. Corolla cries. "Oh, my God!"

Zane peers through a crack in the fence. His jaw drops. "Crap!" he breathes.

I push Zane aside and look for myself. Mr. Corolla has a garden hose, and he's spraying it full blast at something. I squint into the darkness, trying to make out what it is.

A dark, wet form streaks across the yard and scrambles over the fence. I leap to my feet just in time to catch a glimpse of a cat bounding into the bushes.

"I'm outta here!" Zane mutters.

He jumps up and runs to find his bike. We run after him, stumbling over one another as we feel for our bikes in the darkness. Do I have mine? I'm not sure. All I know is it's a bicycle. I drag it into the parking lot behind Mr. Corolla's house and jump on. Then I start pedaling, and I don't stop until I'm home.

I'm riding my bike to school, but my mind is far, far away. I'm thinking about Amigo. He's supposed to come home today. How will he look? Will he be able to walk? Will he even recognize me?

I'm also thinking about Casey and how I'm not going to be able to work on the tree house with him this weekend. That's because my parents grounded me for coming home late last night. I can't complain too much, though. At least they believed my story about going over to Casey's house and forgetting the time. If they knew what I was really up to, they probably would have grounded me for life!

I pass the mini-mart and turn onto School Lane.

Fortunately, Mom didn't hassle me about wearing shorts today. She was too busy yelling at me for forgetting to bring home her pink sweater. She's going to be even madder when she learns the truth. I can't find the dumb thing. It's not in the Lost and Found. It's not in my classroom. It's like it vanished into thin air.

I pass Mr. Corolla's house. There's a big orange cat sitting on his front porch. I look—then look again. The cat has an irregular patch of hair missing from his back. A sick feeling washes over me as I hit the brakes. Did we do that?

"Murphy," I whisper, "I'm sorry."

The cat just looks at me, unblinking.

When I get to school, Casey is waiting at the bike stands. "John," he says anxiously, "I think I set Mr. Corolla's cat on fire."

"I know," I answer. "I saw him. But listen, you can't blame yourself. Everyone threw those firecrackers."

"Everyone except you."

It's true. But that's only because Zane goaded Casey into throwing the last batch. If he'd pressured me to light them, can I say I would have refused? Probably not.

Zane rides up and skids to a stop with Spencer and Ernesto right behind him. He's all fake concern as he asks, "Did you see Old Man Corolla's cat?"

A snicker escapes Spencer's lips. "Dude, that cat is having a bad-hair day!"

The guys burst out laughing.

"It's not funny," Casey snaps. "Those firecrackers set him on fire. He could have died!"

"Lighten up," Zane scoffs. "The cat's fine. Besides, did you see how funny he looked when Old Man Corolla turned the hose on him?"

"Like a wet mop!" Ernesto exclaims.

"A drowned rat!" Spencer adds.

"I almost busted a gut laughing!" Zane declares.

"You weren't laughing," I say. "You were running. We all were."

"Speak for yourself, Frankenstein," Zane shoots back. "Anyway, the point is we got Old Man Corolla back, big time!"

The bell rings, and the boys strut toward the school— all except Casey, who kneels down to do something with his bike. I follow Zane, but my stomach won't settle. I keep imagining Murphy with his hair on fire. Poor guy! He must have been so scared!

The boys' laughter is still ringing in my ears. Is that the way guys are supposed to act? If Rob and Stuart were here, would they be laughing too?

Maybe. I mean, it did look funny when Murphy got soaked—in a crazy, cartoon kind of way. And after all, he wasn't seriously hurt.

So why am I not laughing? I kick a bumpy gray pebble into the grass. Maybe I'll never fit in. Not as a girl. Not as a boy either.

As we walk into the school, I glance around me. I'm surrounded by boys who are supposed to be my friends. Fellow members of the League of SuperDudes. So why do I feel so alone?

3:34 P.M.

"Is he here?" I exclaim, bursting through the front door.

Mom appears in the foyer. "He's in the kitchen, but don't make a lot of noise. He's sleeping."

I follow Mom into the kitchen. My stomach tightens in nervous anticipation. And then I see him—my wild, high-energy mutt, lying on his dog bed, eyes closed, unmoving. He's got one of those plastic funnel-shaped collars around his neck and a three-inch incision on his shaved stomach. The skin around it is red and swollen.

For an instant, I'm sure he's dead. Then he moves his legs a little, as if he's running. It's a low-key version of his usual sleep behavior. Sometimes he even barks in his sleep. I always figured he was dreaming about chasing mice or something.

"What's that?" I ask, pointing to the sheet of plastic under his bed.

"He doesn't have control of his bowels yet," Mom explains. "Remember what we talked about? We're going to have to clean up after him for a while."

Ugh. I'd forgotten about that. "Can't we just take him outside every few hours?"

"Joanie," she says, laying her hands on my shoulders, "you knew it would be like this. We said we'd take care of him together."

The whole togetherness thing was your idea, I want to say. But I stop myself when I realize that Mom is letting Amigo sleep in her kitchen. *Mom,* who normally doesn't even want him in the house!

"Right," I say.

Just then, Amigo lets out a sad little whine. I turn around. His eyes are open and he's trying to stand up. Only problem is his back legs won't cooperate. With a yelp, he falls back on the bed.

I run over and kneel beside him. "Good boy," I say, stroking his head. "Good boy."

Mom sighs. "Dr. McCullough gave me some pain-killers, but I can't get Amigo to take them."

"He's always been terrible with pills."

Mom laughs. "Remember the flea pills?"

I start to giggle. We tried giving Amigo a monthly pill to kill fleas and ticks. No matter what we hid it in— cheese, hot dogs, even chicken—he would spit it out. Finally, we gave up and switched to flea spray.

"There's got to be something we can hide it in," I say. "Something he loves so much he won't even notice."

Mom thinks it over. "Let's check the fridge."

We peer into it together. "Scrambled eggs?" I suggest. "Peanut butter? Brie?"

"Bring them out," Mom says. "Let's see what we can cook up."

"Good God, is that Joanie in an apron?"

I look up to see Rob standing in the doorway. Stuart is right behind him.

"Don't tell me you're trying to get her interested in cooking again, Mom," Stu says.

"I'm not cooking," I protest. "We were trying to come up with something to put Amigo's pain pill in. We found it too."

Mom is kneeling beside Amigo, who is happily licking his chops. "Fried chicken livers smeared with peanut butter," she announces, beaming.

"Disgusting!" Stuart moans.

We hear the front door open. Dad walks in from the foyer. "How's the patient?" Suddenly, he notices the kitchen counters. They're completely covered with food, frying pans, and utensils. "Are we having guests for dinner?"

When Mom tells him we've spent the last two hours cooking for Amigo, he shakes his head. "Didn't Dr.

McCullough show you how to give a pill to a dog? You just hold his muzzle and push it to the back of his tongue. Then you massage his throat until he swallows."

"Maybe you don't remember the flea pills," I say. Dad tried that back-of-the-throat method. Amigo just wiggled out of his grasp. The one time Dad managed to make him swallow, Amigo immediately threw up.

Dad looks blank. "All I'm saying is you went to a lot of trouble for a dog."

Maybe Dad's right. Still, it was kind of fun coming up with all those weird food combinations. We tried a cheese-and-pain-pill omelet, a chicken-skin-and-pain-pill taco, even hamburger-and-pain-pill tartare (that's raw hamburger with anchovies and capers, believe it or not).

Mom smiles sweetly at Dad. "Hon, could you go out and get us some Chinese?"

I can't believe it! Mom is letting us get takeout! This usually happens only when she's too sick to cook.

"Hey, maybe letting Amigo get that operation wasn't such a bad idea after all," Rob says, sneaking a tortilla from the counter.

"Just as long as we don't have to clean up after him," Stu adds.

"You don't have to clean up after Amigo," Mom replies. "Just us. I want you boys to put away all the food on the counters and wash the pans."

They let out an anguished wail. "Unfair!" Stuart moans.

"Get to work," Mom says. "Joanie and I will be in the living room, watching TV."

I grin. Maybe this cooking stuff isn't so bad—not if it means getting a bunch of sweet perks. I take off my apron and toss it at Stuart.

2:00 A.M.

Beep! Beep! Beep!

I hit my alarm clock and look at the time. Two in the morning! I let out a groan and roll over. My bed is so soft and warm. The last thing I want to do is get up. But I told Mom I would give Amigo his next pain pill.

The way I see it, it's the least I can do. Mom got up at midnight to check on him and clean his bed. She'll get up again at four. So the two o'clock watch is mine.

I peel off the covers and put on my robe and slippers. There's a full moon throwing squares of pale blue light on the floor. I shuffle down the hall. I can hear Dad's soft snores coming from the master bedroom.

I pad downstairs and flip on the kitchen light. Oh, my gosh! Amigo's bed is empty!

I check every square inch of the kitchen. Then I run into the garage. He's not there either.

Now I'm getting panicky. I search the living room and the dining room. Then I run upstairs to Mom and Dad's bedroom. I push open the door and step inside. Dad's lying in the bed with one arm thrown over his head, snoring evenly. But where's Mom?

"Over here," a soft voice whispers.

I find Mom sitting on the floor, next to the armoire. Amigo is stretched out beside her. I walk closer and gaze at them in bewilderment.

"I heard a noise in the hall about half an hour ago," she whispers. "It was Amigo. I guess he was looking for us. Poor guy, he was pretty shaky. He almost walked into the wall."

I chuckle softly. Amigo couldn't even get up a few hours ago. Now he's walking—or at least trying to. "The pain pills must be working."

"A spoonful of chicken liver helps the medicine go down," Mom warbles.

I giggle and sit down beside her. "I've never seen Amigo in your bedroom before."

"Well, what's the alternative? I can't let him wander around the house. He might rip his stitches."

She's trying to look stern, but when she strokes Amigo's head, I know she doesn't mean it. "Thanks, Mom," I say.

Just then, I hear a soft *ffft* from Amigo's hind quarters. Something wet and smelly drips onto the rug. I gasp and cover my nose with my hand. So gross!

Amigo stirs, opens one eye, then goes back to sleep. I

look to Mom. *What now?* She gets up without a word. A minute later, she's back with a spray bottle of rug cleaner and a sponge.

"Can't let your father know about this," she whispers as she sprays and rubs. Soon the gross smell is replaced by a lemony one. She sits back down, smiling so sweetly you'd think nothing ever happened.

We sit there for a while in silence, just petting Amigo and watching him sleep. I glance over at Mom. In the moonlight, her face looks even more beautiful than usual. I've seen that face looking down at *me* at night, stroking *my* hair. She always sits up with my brothers and me when we're sick. She cooks special food for us and reads to us, too. If she has to, she even cleans up our messes.

"My father died when I was fifteen," Mom says quietly. "I've told you that, right?"

I nod.

"He'd had a heart attack. The doctor did bypass surgery and sent him home with pages of instructions. He was supposed to stop smoking, exercise, go on a special diet. But I think the stay in the hospital just did him in. When he came home, he was a different man from the one I'd known. He looked worn out, defeated. Like he'd given up."

"You mean he didn't do the things the doctor told him?" I ask.

"Not with any consistency." She looks away. "He died six months later."

I frown, thinking it over. It just seems so crazy. He had a wife and kids. How could he give up?

Mom turns to me. "I'm different. I'm a fighter. If there's even the tiniest chance of winning, I won't give up."

"You?" I say with surprise. "A fighter?"

Now she's the one who looks surprised. "You'd better believe it. When I want something, I won't take no for an answer."

I think it over. I remember the time Rob didn't get into the honors math class he wanted. Mom practically camped out in the principal's office until he changed his mind. And that time Dad got sued by one of his patients. Mom worked morning, noon, and night, organizing his papers and gathering research for the trial. She barely slept until his name was cleared.

"I think you're a lot like me," Mom says, brushing a strand of hair off my forehead. "You're a fighter too."

I think about the way I play football—all out. And the way I hung from the tree at the preserve. When I looked down at that ravine, I wanted to turn back. But I didn't.

Then I think about how I didn't want to give up on Amigo. That was a whole different kind of fighting. It wasn't physical, like football, but it still meant hanging tough and not taking the easy way out.

I look at Mom. She didn't want to give up on Amigo

either. Now she's taking care of him, even though it means getting hair on her clothes and poop on the rugs. Even though she knows it might not work and Amigo might die.

Hmm. It's hard to believe, but maybe Mom and I have something in common after all.

It's Sunday night, and I'm in the bathroom, brushing my teeth before bed. I look at myself in the mirror. The pixie curls are in front of my ears. I smile and cock my head, the way Mom does when she's talking to Dad. I look like a girl. I'm Joanie.

Then I rake the curls behind my ears. I hook my thumbs in the waistband of my jeans and smirk the way Zane did when he threw the firecrackers into Mr. Corolla's backyard. I look like a boy. I'm John.

One is what Mom wants. The other is what the SuperDudes want. But neither one feels quite right. I mess up my hair and blow a raspberry at the kid in the mirror. Why is everything so confusing?

I hear a thumping sound and look around. Amigo is standing in the doorway, wagging his tail. He looks a bit unsteady on his feet, but he's upright—a big improvement over how he looked two days ago. In fact, today he ate some of his regular dog food and took a short walk in the backyard. He even made a feeble lunge at a squirrel!

I rinse my mouth and lean down to scratch him behind the ear. Rob appears at the top of the stairs, his skateboard under his arm. "How's the Wonder Dog?" he asks, stopping to give him a pat.

"He took his pain pill tonight with only a little peanut butter on it," I reply. "I think he's starting to like it."

"Oh, great," Rob groans. "More chicken livers for us." He shoots me a grin as he walks into his room.

I grin back. Now that Amigo is past the pooping-in-the-house stage, my brothers are giving him a lot more attention. Even Dad's been stopping to scratch him and ask, "How's the patient?"

Then last night after dinner, I overheard Mom and Dad talking in the kitchen. "Dr. McCullough said the biopsy didn't show any sign of cancer outside the tumor margins," Dad was saying.

"Amigo's a tough old mutt," Mom replied. "I think he's going to make it."

"He's certainly got the prettiest nurse around," Dad said in a syrupy voice.

I stopped eavesdropping when I heard the first smack. Mom and Dad are always making kissy-face in the kitchen. It's totally disgusting!

Now I leave the bathroom and walk back to my room. Amigo follows and looks longingly at my bed. With his stitches, he can't quite make the jump, so he curls up on the floor instead.

"Don't worry," I say. "You'll be better soon."

Of course, when he's better, Mom probably won't let him sleep in my room anymore.

"But there'll be other perks," I tell him. "Like walks in the preserve."

I smile. My parents didn't let me go there on Saturday because I was grounded. But today I begged and begged, and they finally caved. Maybe it's because I've been so helpful with Amigo. I didn't ask. I just got on my bike and took off.

Casey was there, working on the tree house. He was cutting some two-by-fours, so he showed me how to use a saw. We even made a door with real hinges, and Casey showed me how to screw them in. I think I'm really getting the hang of this tool thing. I might even trying building a birdhouse for the backyard.

While Casey and I worked, I gave him the update on Amigo. Then we told jokes.

"Mommy, Mommy, when are we having Aunt Edna for dinner?"

"Shut up and eat. We haven't finished your grandmother yet."

A man was ice fishing, but he couldn't seem to catch anything. Then a boy came along, cut a hole in the ice, and caught six fish in a row.

"How do you do it, kid?" the man asked.

The kid said, "Roo raf ro reep rur rums rarm."

"What?" the man said.

"Roo raf ro reep rur rums rarm."

"I can't understand a word you're saying," the man said.

So the kid spit something into his hand and said, "You have to keep your worms warm."

Casey laughed so hard that snot flew out of his nose. When he finally quieted down, he wiped his nose on his sleeve and gazed out through the branches of the tree. I figured he was trying to think of another joke, until he said, "All this talk about pets is making me think about Mr. Corolla's cat."

"Murphy's going to be okay," I said. "He just lost some hair, that's all. It'll grow back."

"I know. But still . . ." He shrugged. "I'm thinking I

should go to Mr. Corolla and confess. I could use my allowance to pay back his vet bill a little each week."

I looked at Casey with awe. It would take a lot of courage to face up to Mr. Corolla. Not the kind of courage it took to throw the firecrackers either. This would be different and probably a lot harder.

Casey looked at me expectantly. I think he was hoping for some encouragement, but, instead, I turned away. It was partly because I didn't know what to say. I mean, if Zane had been there, he would have ragged Casey mercilessly for being such a wimp. Shouldn't I do the same? And yet, what I really wanted to do was give Casey a hug and ask if I could go with him to Mr. Corolla's house. What was wrong with me?

But that wasn't the only reason I turned away. Casey's confession had made me wish I could confess too.

I opened my mouth, then closed it again. Casey wasn't like the other guys. He was funny and easy to talk to. If I told him my big secret, maybe he'd understand.

But what if he didn't? What if he thought I was ridiculous? Or worse yet, some kind of freak? What if he ran to the guys and told them everything? Then the whole school would know the truth—John is really Joan. I'd never live it down!

Mom's voice brings me back to the present. "Joanie, bedtime," she calls from the hallway. "You have school tomorrow."

"Okay, okay." I start taking off my clothes, but I'm still thinking about Casey. Did I do the right thing? As I'm pulling off my T-shirt, my arm gets caught in the sleeve and bumps against my chest. Strange—something feels sore. I look down and—

No! It can't be! My chest isn't flat as a chalkboard anymore. I've got breasts—well, the beginning of them, anyway.

My head is spinning. I run back to the bathroom and stare at myself in the mirror. No doubt about it. Where there was once nothing, there are now little lumps.

Am I supposed to be happy? Sad? All I feel is confused—and a little scared. I mean, what else is going to change? And how am I going to hide it all from the kids at school?

"Joanie," Mom calls, her voice sounding closer with every word, "I thought I told you to get into bed."

The bathroom door starts to open. I gasp and pull down my pajama top.

"What's wrong?" Mom asks. "You look like you just saw a ghost."

Everything is wrong! I want to scream. *Absolutely everything!*

But how can I explain my feelings to Mom? She doesn't even think I should be wearing skater shorts to school. If she knew what was really going on, she'd probably have a stroke!

"Nothing's wrong," I say, forcing a smile. "Nothing at all."

SUPERKID
in
"The Telltale Sign"

by John Frankenhauser

I was walking through the city, on my way to the skateboard park. In my skater shorts and T-shirt, everyone thought I was a normal kid. They didn't know I was SuperKid, crime fighter and leader of the League of SuperDudes.

Suddenly, something hit me from behind. Everything went black, and when I woke up, I was lying inside a van, surrounded by Dr. Dread's cyborg rats. I gasped and tried to sit up, but I couldn't move. Leather straps bound my arms and legs.

"You'll pay for this!" I cried.

"It is you who shall pay," a voice said. The rats stepped back, and Dr. Dread appeared at my bedside. "How do you like my new mobile laboratory?" he asked with a cruel smile.

"The SuperDudes will find me," I warned. "They'll destroy every one of you."

"They won't have to find you," he said, "because

I'm setting you free right now. But first," he added, pointing to my right hand, "tell me how you like your new tattoo."

I lifted my head to stare at my hand. It had been tattooed with Dr. Dread's logo—a skull, two test tubes, and the letters DD. I let out a scream. I was marked with the sign of evil!

Dr. Dread laughed. "I used a new chemically altered ink—invented by me, of course. The ink will slowly seep into your blood and sap your superpowers. Soon Superkid will be just a plain old nobody!"

Dr. Dread leaned over and untied the leather straps. Then the rats shoved me out the back of the van. I scrambled to my feet as the van pulled away.

Hopping on my superpowered skateboard, I chased after Dr. Dread. As I rode, I pulled out my mini-boomerang. I reared back and aimed at the van's tires. But when I threw, the boomerang fell short.

Oh, no! My powers were fading already! I kicked off, trying to make my skateboard go faster. But Dr. Dread's van was getting farther and farther ahead of me. I watched helplessly as it disappeared around a corner.

What now? I couldn't face the other superheroes with my shameful tattoo. The only solution was to wear gloves. But how could I hide my failing superpowers? If I wanted to be part of the League of SuperDudes, I knew I had to find a way.

At first, everything went fine. The gloves hid my tattoo. And since Dr. Dread and his rats were laying low, there was no reason for me to use my super-powers.

Then one day the Porcupine, the Blade, Toolbox, and Slime Boy—my partners in the League of SuperDudes—rode to my house on their supercharged BMX mini-bikes. Toolbox—known as Casey when he wasn't in his superhero costume—found me in my room, playing video games.

"Dr. Dread was spotted catching frogs in the creek behind his laboratory," he said.

"He's up to no good," I said. "I'll bet my life on it."

Suddenly, I noticed Toolbox looking at my hand. Oh, no! I wasn't wearing my gloves! Quickly, I whipped my hand behind my back. But it was too late.

"What's that?" he demanded, reaching behind me to grab my hand.

I tried to struggle, but with my weakening super-powers, I was no match for him. When he saw the tattoo, his face went white.

"How did this happen?" he asked.

Reluctantly, I told him the whole story. "Without my superpowers, who am I?" I asked, hanging my head. "I'm no good to anyone. I'm nothing."

"Curse you, Dr. Dread!" Toolbox cried, shaking his fist at the sky. "You'll pay for this!"

"Tell the SuperDudes to keep fighting," I said. "As for me, I'm going away where no one knows me."

"No," Toolbox said. "Even without your superpowers, you can still help us fight Dr. Dread."

"But how?" I asked.

"All it takes is intelligence and courage, and you've got tons of both." He reached for my tattooed hand. "Come with us, SuperKid. Come with us and fight."

Was Toolbox right? Did I still have something to offer? I wanted to believe him, but I just wasn't sure.

"I'll think it over," I said at last.

Toolbox could tell I needed to be alone. With a final squeeze of my tattooed hand, he left to join the waiting SuperDudes. My heart was heavy as I stood at the window, watching them ride away.

Would I ever ride with my comrades again? I just didn't know.

October 8

8:40 A.M.

"Class," Ms. Anstine says, "before you open your reading books, I have an announcement to make. Next week there will be a special health-education assembly called Growing and Changing: Your Body and You."

"My big brother told me about this," Hailey whispers to Lucinda. "It's sex education!"

My eyes grow wide. Sex education! It sounds embarrassing—and extremely interesting.

"It's nothing we don't already know," Lucinda whispers back. "Just menstruation and stuff."

Menstruation? I think Mom gave me a book about that

at the end of the summer, but I didn't read it. Come to think of it, I don't even know where it is.

Suddenly, Hailey notices me looking at her. She blushes and hisses, "Mind your own business, John."

"The boys will have their assembly on Monday," Ms. Anstine continues, "and the girls will go on Tuesday. On Wednesday we'll all see a film called *Boys and Girls: Celebrating Our Similarities and Respecting Our Differences.*"

"I know about Lucinda's differences," Zane whispers. "Both of them."

The boys snicker, all except me. I'm too busy thinking about those assemblies. I'll be going with the boys, of course. I'll probably learn a lot of interesting stuff too. But what will I be missing? Will it be something important that girls need to know? Something about menstruation or about those lumps on my chest?

"All right, all right," Ms. Anstine says with a smile, "I know this is a subject that makes kids giggle. But it's a good movie, I promise."

"Is it R-rated?" Spencer asks.

Ms. Anstine ignores him. "Oh, I almost forgot. I think you all know that the school's Fall Festival is coming up in a couple of weeks. I've got flyers to pass out."

Fall Festival? I haven't heard a word about it. I look quizzically at Casey.

"There's games like Dunk-the-Principal," he whispers.

"And the PTA has a bake sale with killer brownies."

Bake sale? Uh-oh. My mom loves stuff like that. She always donates some fancy homemade pastry like napoleons. She usually volunteers at the table, too.

Normally, I wouldn't care. But this year is different. If Mom starts hanging out with the other mothers, pretty soon someone's bound to ask who her kid is. What will happen when she says, "Joanie Frankenhauser," and some other mother asks, "Don't you mean John?"

The thought is too horrible to contemplate. When Casey passes the stack of flyers to me, I take mine and stuff it in the back of my desk. No way can I let Mom find out about the Fall Festival. Of course, that means I'll probably have to miss it too. I'm not happy about that—especially when I think of the fun I would have had with Casey—but, well, I guess that's just how it has to be.

12:13 P.M.

"You ready for the third test, SuperDudes?" Zane asks as we sit down at the lunch table.

"Bring it on," Spencer answers.

Zane waits until we're all listening. Then he waits some more. Just when we're about to burst with anticipation, he says, "We follow Lucinda home, surround her, and snap her bra."

I feel my mouth fall open. Zane is so mean! The other guys look equally stunned, all except Spencer, who grins and says, "You're a genius, Hamilton."

"I am, aren't I?" he says with a chuckle.

"I'm out," Ernesto announces. "My sister is good friends with Lucinda. If I do something like that, Lucinda will tell Mari, who will tell my parents, who will whup my butt."

Zane looks at Ernesto like he's looking at a piece of toilet paper on the bottom of his shoe. "Get lost, Ardo," he says. "Go sit with Miguel and the other wimps."

No one speaks. No one moves. Does Zane mean what I think he means? Is he really throwing Ernesto out of the SuperDudes? I can't believe it.

"Come on, man," Ernesto says, laughing uncomfortably. "I passed the other tests, didn't I?"

"I said three tests," Zane answers. He holds up three fingers. "You can count, can't you?"

"So give me something else to do. I just can't mess with Lucinda. You know how it is."

"Yeah, I know how it is," Zane says. "I know you're out of the SuperDudes. I know you're a pathetic wuss."

"I'm not a wuss!" Ernesto cries.

"Sissy!" Spencer taunts, glancing at Zane to see if he approves.

Zane grins. "I think I know why he doesn't want to snap Lucinda's bra. It's 'cause he's a girl, just like her."

If only he knew, I think. *The only girl at this table is me!*

But before I can take the thought any further, Ernesto jumps to his feet. "Take that back!" he snarls.

"Make me," Zane replies.

Ernesto takes a step forward, but Spencer sticks out his foot and trips him. Ernesto stumbles against his chair and falls to the floor with a thud.

The kids at the nearby tables don't know what's going on. All they know is Ernesto fell down. They nudge each other and laugh.

Ernesto's neck is red, and the color is rising like mercury in a thermometer. I look at his face. His eyes are wet and threatening to overflow.

"Look, he's bawling!" Spencer exclaims.

"See, I told you he's a girl," says Zane.

Ernesto scrambles to his feet and hurriedly wipes his eyes. "I'll get you for this," he sputters.

Zane laughs. "Ooh, I'm scared."

Ernesto grabs his tray and stumbles to Miguel's table. I watch him go. My stomach hurts, like somebody just punched me. I never knew boys could be so cruel.

I try to imagine what Ernesto is feeling right now. Like an outcast, I guess. Like a loser who couldn't make the grade. I have a sudden urge to go over and comfort him. But then the guys would think I'm an even bigger wimp than Ernesto, right?

Zane turns to us. "Well, I guess it's just us now. Anyone else want to chicken out?"

"Not me," Spencer says immediately.

I glance at Casey, but he won't meet my eye. *What's he thinking?* I wonder. What am *I* thinking? All I know is I'm scared. I don't want Zane to treat me the way he treated Ernesto. In fact, I think I'd do pretty much anything to avoid it.

But snap Lucinda's bra? Would I really do that?

I just don't know.

2:34 P.M.

"Here she comes," Zane says, grinning as he nudges Spencer.

We're standing by the flagpole. Just the four of us— Zane, Spencer, Casey, and me. The toughest of the tough. The baddest of the bad. The League of SuperDudes.

So why do I feel so scared? So worried? So confused?

I want to talk to Casey so bad, but there hasn't been a chance all afternoon. Or is he just avoiding me? I keep glancing at him, but he won't look back. He's staring down at his shoes like he's staring into a Game Boy screen.

Lucinda, Hailey, and Miranda walk past, talking and laughing. For the first time since I came to Yardville, I find myself wishing I was walking with them instead of standing under the flagpole with the guys.

I try to remember why I thought I was so different from the girls in my class. Okay, I've never been a giggly girly-girl like Hailey and Miranda. But what about Lucinda? Right here, right now, it seems the two of us are more alike than we are different. We both like sports. And pretty soon we'll both be wearing bras.

"How are we going to get Lucinda alone?" Spencer asks.

"No problem," Zane replies. "They split up at the corner."

He waits until the girls are about ten paces ahead of us; then he starts walking. We fall in beside him. My legs feel a little unsteady and my palms are damp. I rub them on the sides of my jeans and remind myself to keep breathing.

In . . . out . . . in . . . out . . .

All I have to do is pass this one last test and I'll be a SuperDude. Just like in my stories, I'll be tough, strong, fearless. I'll be one of the guys.

It's what I've always wanted.

Or is it?

I thought boys had it easy. But hanging around with Zane hasn't been easy at all. I feel like I'm being tested every minute. Any sign of weakness and he'll be on me like a wolf on a lamb.

Is this what all boys have to deal with? I never thought I'd say it, but, man, I feel sorry for them.

"There they go," Zane says as Lucinda waves good-bye to her friends. They turn right; she turns left.

We turn too, following Lucinda up Makefield Avenue.

She walks a couple of blocks and then cuts across an empty lot.

Zane puts out his arm, holding us back. He looks around to see if anyone's watching. There's no one in sight. Just Lucinda, walking through the ankle-high grass and weeds.

Zane waits until she's about halfway across the lot, near a patch of thick bushes. "Now!" he cries.

He starts to run. Spencer runs with him. Casey and I bring up the rear. Lucinda hears our footsteps and turns around. She gasps as Zane and Spencer grab her arms.

"What are you doing?" she cries, struggling to break free. "Let me go!"

This is it—the perfect moment to snap her bra and hightail it out of there. But, instead, Zane drags Lucinda into the bushes. Spencer follows. I hesitate, wondering what's going on. I glance over at Casey. He looks as startled and bewildered as I feel.

"Long as we're here," Zane says with a smirk, "let's see what color it is."

I feel panic rising in my throat. Is Zane nuts? What does he think he's doing?

Spencer holds Lucinda while Zane pulls up her blouse. I feel like it's me he's touching. Like Lucinda, I feel myself tensing. I want to run away. I want to scream.

Then Lucinda does scream, and suddenly I'm running at Zane like the only thing between me and a Super Bowl win is sacking this sucker. I hit him hard, and he falls back into the grass with me on top of him.

"What's the matter with you, Frankenstein?" he sputters, fighting to push me off of him.

"Nothing's the matter with me," I shoot back. "You're the one who's acting like a jerk!"

With a grunt, he shoves me off and jumps to his feet.

"I thought you were okay," he snarls, standing over me. "But you're just like Ernesto. You're a wuss! A sissy! A *girl!*"

He says it like it's the worst insult in the world. There was a time when I might have agreed with him. But now? I glance over at Lucinda. She's watching me like she can't quite figure me out. Maybe it's time to set her straight. It's time to set everyone straight.

"That's right," I say, scrambling to my feet. "I'm a girl."

"What are you talking about?" Zane asks with a frown.

"You heard me. I've just been pretending to be a boy. Actually my name is Joanie. I'm a *girl!*"

Everyone stares at me like I just told them I'm from outer space. I don't care. All I want to do is get out of there. But I can't leave Lucinda.

"Come on," I say, waving her toward me.

Zane doesn't argue. Neither do Spencer or Casey. They're too shocked, I guess. Spencer steps back, and Lucinda hurries out of the bushes. We start walking away, just the two of us, leaving the boys standing there, slack-jawed and speechless.

We're almost to the street on the far side of the vacant lot when Lucinda asks, "Are you really a girl?"

I nod.

"But . . . but why did you tell everyone your name was John?"

"I didn't. It was on the class list that way. I just went with it." I shrug. "It's a long story."

She looks at me, trying to make sense of things. I don't think it's working. Finally, she gives up and says, "Thanks, Joh—I mean, Joanie." She shoots me a quick shy smile and walks away.

I watch until she turns the corner. Then I glance back at the boys. They're still standing by the bushes, looking like they've been turned to stone.

Finally, the spell ends and Zane shakes his fist at me. "I'll get you for this, Frankenstein!"

"Yeah," Spencer adds. "You're dead meat!"

I should be worried. But for some strange reason, I couldn't care less. In fact, I feel excited. Elated, almost. Like my team just won the big game.

Grinning, I turn my back on the boys and start for home.

October 9

3:10 P.M.

"Come on, boy. Let's do it!"

It's Amigo's first trip to the preserve since his surgery, and he's raring to go. Normally, after a day of being cooped up at school, I'd feel the same. But right now I'm not sure where I want to be. Sitting in the tree house? Hiding in my room? Maybe stowed away on a steamer to Madagascar?

All I know is I want to be far, far away from the kids at school, especially Zane Hamilton and his jackass friends.

I climb on my bike and start pedaling—more slowly than usual because Amigo still isn't moving as fast as he used to. When we reach the preserve, I set him free. He sniffs the grass and tries a few experimental stiff-legged hops. He doesn't catch any mice, and I'm kind of glad. After today, I'm not in the mood to watch some innocent creature be hunted down and ripped to shreds.

I don't want to think about it, but the memories keep flooding into my head. Zane and his buddies waiting at the edge of the school grounds for me to show up. The menacing smirk on Zane's face. The harsh voices taunting me.

"Whaddaya think—is it a girl or a boy?"

"Both."

"Neither."

"It's a mutant!"

"A freak!"

"Hey, Frankenstein, why don't you show us what you've got? Then we'll know for sure."

I kept pedaling, just the way I'm pedaling toward the Stiegman Street entrance now. I look around for Casey. He's nowhere in sight, thank goodness. I drop my bike and climb up into the tree house. It's quiet up there. Just the chirping of birds and the cool breeze rustling the leaves. I reach out and touch a trembling leaf. The edges are red—a sure sign that autumn is finally here.

More memories. Zane raising his hand as we all take our seats. "Ms. Anstine, John Frankenhauser isn't really a boy. She told me yesterday she's actually a girl!"

All eyes were on me. Everyone looked stunned, except

Ms. Anstine. "Is that so?" she asked, a smile playing across her lips.

"Yes," I admitted. "My name was wrong on the roster and . . . and I just went along with it. My real name is Joan. Joanie. Uh, that's my nickname."

"Welcome to Yardville, Joanie," Ms. Anstine said cheerily, just the way she did on the first day of school. Then she addressed the class. "Turn to page two-ten in your reading book. Who'd like to read the first paragraph out loud?"

I could have hugged her. I could have done it again when the recess bell rang and she said, "Joanie, could I have a word with you?"

All right! Now I wouldn't have to face the stares and questions of my classmates—at least not immediately. Best of all, I wouldn't have to face Zane.

My relief faded when I realized I *did* have to face Ms. Anstine. But she was amazingly cool about the whole thing. "I'm going to have to tell your parents, you know," she said matter-of-factly.

I nodded. They'd find out eventually, anyway; I was pretty sure of that. Zane would definitely shoot off his mouth at the Fall Festival.

"I don't think what happened is an indication of any serious psychological problems," Ms. Anstine went on, "and I don't want your parents to think that either. I mean, unless I'm reading this wrong. What do you think, Joanie?"

"Yes—no. I mean, whatever you said," I answered quickly.

She laughed. "Okay, but you've got to do something for me. First of all, can you tell me what you learned from your experience?"

My mind was reeling. What *had* I learned? What did she want to hear? "Uh, lies are bad?" I suggested.

She looked disappointed. "You can do better than that, Joanie. I want you to think about it—really think—and then put something down on paper. A journal entry, an essay, a SuperKid story, whatever. Just promise me you'll write about what happened, and promise me you'll let me see it when you're finished."

"Okay," I said. "I promise."

She smiled. "Do you want to go out to recess now?"

"Not really."

"Here's some paper. Sit down and start writing."

I took the paper. That's when I noticed the pink sweater on the back of Ms. Anstine's chair.

"Where did you get that sweater?" I asked.

She turned and looked at it. "This? I found it lying on the floor of the classroom. I should have taken it to the Lost and Found, but I was chilly, so I put it on. I guess I forgot about it."

I smiled. I knew Mom was going to be pleased.

* * *

Now I glance over the edge of the tree house, making sure Casey hasn't shown up. All clear. I sit down with my back against the tree.

Immediately, my head fills with memories of second recess. It was everything I'd been dreading. Zane was back with his old posse—Spencer, Ernesto, even Miguel. They surrounded me and got to it.

"Is that a boy in a girl's shirt or a girl in boy's pants?"

"It's SuperKid!"

"Super*Freak* is more like it!"

Only Casey was missing. As I turned my back on the boys, I scanned the playground for him. I finally spotted him on the swings—a spot the big kids usually avoided as being too babyish. He was pumping hard, sailing toward the clouds. I watched, wishing I was swinging with him.

But would he want me there beside him? He wasn't hassling me like Zane and the crew. But he wasn't making an effort to talk to me either.

Zane and his friends were still trashing me. I remembered yesterday's plan to tell them I went undercover on purpose, just to find out what it was like to be a boy. Or better yet, to spy on the boys and learn all their secrets.

But suddenly, lying seemed kind of pointless. I'd embarrassed Zane yesterday when I pushed him away from Lucinda, so now he had to get back at me. I'd learned enough about boys—well, boys like Zane, at least—to know that's just the way it worked. And nothing I said or did was going to change it.

So instead of trying, I turned my back on them and wandered over to the drinking fountain. Kids were nudging each other and pointing as I walked past. I could hear their giggles as I leaned down to drink.

"Hey," said a girl's voice behind me.

I stood up. It was Lucinda.

"Hi," I replied with a weak smile.

"Don't worry," she said. "Everyone will forget all about this in a couple of weeks. Of course, you won't be able to play ball with the boys anymore."

"I know." I hesitated, trying to find the courage to speak. "So, uh, maybe you and I could shoot hoops together sometime." I motioned toward the baskets.

She shrugged. "Yeah, maybe." Then she walked away.

Now, sitting in the tree house, I let out a ragged sigh. Will Lucinda's "maybe" ever turn into a "yes"? Or will I spend the rest of the year alone?

Well, I remind myself, it's not as if I haven't experienced *that* before. Still, after a week of being in with the boys—of playing football and basketball every recess—it's definitely going to take some getting used to.

Suddenly, I hear a noise below me. With my heart in my throat, I leap up and look over the edge of the tree house. It's Casey, and he's climbing up!

I panic. For an instant, I seriously consider running to

the other side and jumping out. Then Casey looks up, and our eyes meet. He looks away fast, hesitates, then continues climbing.

I reconsider my jumping idea. I don't think I'd enjoy spending the year in a body cast. Finally, I sit back down. Casey appears a moment later. He climbs into the tree house and plops down across from me.

Nobody moves. Nobody speaks.

"Why'd you do it?" he asks at last, staring down at the laces of his Nikes. "I feel like a moron, thinking how you tricked me."

My heart sinks. He thinks I did it as a joke, just to fool people and make them look stupid. To make *him* look stupid.

"I didn't set out to trick anyone," I answer. "It's like I said in class. Ms. Anstine called my name wrong and I didn't correct her. Then I didn't know how to get out of it. Besides," I admit, "I didn't want to."

"Why not?" he asks with a puzzled frown.

"Because I didn't want to be a girl anymore. I mean, I thought boys had it easy. They don't have to dress up or look pretty or act sweet." I shrugged. "But now . . . well, I don't know. It's just not that simple."

Casey snorts a laugh. "Being a guy is no walk in the park. All that suck-it-up, boys-don't-cry stuff is hard to live up to—especially with dudes like Zane on your back."

"I didn't realize how hard it would be," I admit. "But I wanted to be accepted so bad, I went along with it."

"Yeah, I know what you mean. But here's the weird part—you're much better at being macho than me. You never backed down on the football field. And you climbed that oak tree like it was a jungle gym." He glances over at me, looking half-irritated, half-impressed. "You're one tough girl."

I laugh. It's been awhile since I've done that, and it feels good. "Thanks," I say. "But there are other kinds of tough."

I'm thinking about my mother, cleaning up after Amigo. I'm thinking about Casey too.

"Did you talk to Mr. Corolla?" I ask.

He rolls his eyes. "He was so mad, I thought he was going to call the cops. But in the end, we worked out a deal. He wouldn't take my allowance money. He wants me to do odd jobs around the house to pay back the vet bill."

"It took guts to face up to him," I point out.

Casey shrugs. "I guess. But what about you? You stood up to Zane when he was hassling Lucinda. That took a lot more courage than I'll ever have."

"You don't have the guts to stand up to Zane?" I ask. "Then what was going on at recess today? Why weren't you hanging with him and his crew?"

"He was making fun of you! I wasn't going to do that. You're my friend."

I shoot him a teasing smile. "Even though I'm a girl?"

He nods.

"A girl who can play football better than you?"

He laughs, then nods again.

"You're my friend too," I tell him.

"Even though I'm a boy?" he asks, crossing his arms across his chest. "A boy who can bake cookies better than you?"

"So what are we saying?" I ask, suddenly perplexed. "That boys can do anything they want, and so can girls?"

He shrugs. "I guess."

"But then that means there's no difference between us. We're exactly the same."

Casey frowns and stretches out his legs. "There's got to be a difference. I mean, look at us—we're not twins!"

I think about my new formfitting T—and about what's underneath. Suddenly, my cheeks grow hot and my skin starts to tingle. I sneak a quick glance at Casey. My heart practically stops dead when I realize he's sneaking a glance at me.

Breathe, I tell myself. *Breathe!* It isn't working. I'm going to faint, I just know it!

Then all at once I know what to do.

"Did you hear about the frog who called the Psychic Hot Line?" I ask. "The psychic told him he was going to meet a young woman who would want to know every-thing about him. 'Will I meet her at a party?' the frog asked. 'No,' the psychic said. 'You'll meet her next term—in her biology class!'"

Casey laughs so hard that he chokes, and I have to pound him on the back. Finally, he says, "You're okay, Frankenstein. But things might get a little weird if we stay friends. I mean, we're not a couple of guys hanging out anymore. I'm a guy and you're . . . you know, a girl."

"You say it like I have a disease or something," I scoff. "Look, don't think I'm going to start acting different, Dilliplane. I can still kick your butt on a football field."

Casey is about to reply when all at once we hear Amigo start to bark. Casey jumps to his feet, and I notice some pieces of paper sticking out of his back pocket.

"What's that?" I ask, pointing.

He feels his back pocket and shrugs. "I've been working on the illustrations for your story. They're not very good, but . . ."

I grab them out of his pocket and look them over. "Not very good?" I shout. "They're awesome!"

Casey grins. "We can still put together that book if you want."

Amigo's still barking, a high-pitched yelp that could break glass. I look down at him. When he sees me, he puts his front paws on the trunk of the maple tree and whines pitifully.

"Ever since his operation, he wants to be with me twenty-four-seven," I explain.

"Hey, I've got an idea," Casey says. "We can build a platform with a pulley system and hoist him up here."

"You can do that?" I ask incredulously.

"*We* can do it. I'll teach you." He grins. "We'll start tomorrow."

Tomorrow? My stomach twists into a pretzel. Tomorrow there'll be more stares, more whispering, more teasing. And when Ms. Anstine calls my parents—oh, man! I don't even want to think about it!

But tomorrow isn't here yet. I look at Casey—sweet, funny, forgiving Casey. And then I realize that for the first time in a long, long while, I'm not thinking about what it means to be a girl *or* a boy. I'm just happy to be me: Joan Rebecca Frankenhauser. Casey's best friend.

SUPERKID
in
"A Brand-New Day"

by Joanie R. Frankenhauser

Days had passed since I'd sadly watched the SuperDudes ride away from my house. Hour after hour, I sat alone in my room, mourning the loss of my superpowers. No longer could I fling a Frisbee at the speed of light or power my skateboard through Dr. Dread's ion force field. In fact, my athletic ability was no greater than that of the average kid.

My life as a superhero was over. And yet, I could not forget Toolbox's words: "All it takes is intelligence and courage, and you have tons of both."

I wanted to believe him, but what if it wasn't enough? In fact, what if my presence on the battlefield actually put the other SuperDudes in danger? If something bad happened to them because of me, I'd never forgive myself.

Then one day, I was in my room playing a video game to pass the time. Suddenly, I knew how to beat the level. It just came to me in a flash of inspi-

146

ration. I continued playing. The game, which had seemed so unbeatable, was now simple to me. Within minutes, I'd mastered the highest level. Piece of cake!

What was going on? I took out my homework and finished it in five minutes. Then I opened a book of puzzles. I whizzed through them.

Incredible! My super-athletic ability was gone, but it had been replaced by super-intelligence! And then, like an electric light turning on, I realized something. I had never seen Zane—the Porcupine—and Dr. Dread together in the same place. In fact, whenever Dr. Dread was around, the Porcupine seemed to disappear.

What did it mean? I knew I had to find out.

I rounded up the League of SuperDudes, and we drove to Dr. Dread's lab. The ion force field was gone and so was the electric fence. We walked right in. But the abandoned warehouse was empty.

"Let's split up and look around," the Porcupine suggested.

I went north. Toolbox went south. The Blade went east. Slime Boy went west. The Porcupine headed for the roof to make sure no one was hiding up there.

I walked into Dr. Dread's laboratory. Behind the tables of test tubes and beakers was a chalkboard covered with equations. With my brand-new super-intelligence, they were easy to understand. I realized immediately that Dr. Dread had created a mini-computer that could be fitted into a mask and controlled by facial muscles.

Suddenly, a voice cried, "Get him!"

I spun around to see Dr. Dread and his army of cyborg rats running toward me. Oh, no! Without my super-athletic ability, how would I stop them from destroying me?

My only chance was to get to Dr. Dread. With my heart in my throat, I zigzagged between the rats. One of them knocked me down with his hairy paw, but I leaped to my feet. I couldn't run very fast, but I was determined to keep going. A rat grabbed me and bit my arm with his pointy teeth, but I wrenched myself free. I zigzagged around two attacking rats and scrambled between another rat's legs.

Finally, I cornered Dr. Dread behind his lab table. "Call off the rats," I ordered.

He just laughed. "Give up, SuperKid. You've lost your superpowers. You're as good as dead!"

I stared into his evil face. He grinned with cruel delight. But why was his skin so stiff? It was barely moving.

Suddenly, I understood! With a shout of triumph, I

lunged at Dr. Dread. My fingers closed around the skin on his flabby cheeks. I pulled with all my might.

With a loud rip, his face came off in my hands, revealing his true identity. Dr. Dread was actually Zane Hamilton!

"No!" he wailed, hiding his face in his hands.

I gazed down at the mask. Inside it was the mini-computer that controlled the cyborg rats. I flung it against the floor. It smashed into a million pieces.

To my amazement, the rats turned on Zane. "Stop!" he shrieked. "It's SuperKid you're supposed to attack, not me!"

But the rats were no longer programmed to obey their leader, and I guess they were tired of being bossed around. So tired, in fact, that they wanted revenge.

Squeaking with fiendish delight, they fell on Zane with a vengeance. Within seconds, they had ripped him limb from limb and were chewing on his bloody bones.

The SuperDudes heard the noise and ran into the room. When they saw the rats down on all fours, squeaking tamely, they were stunned. Quickly, I told them what had happened.

"With Dr. Dread out of the picture, the city is safe," I said. "Let's go home and return to our normal lives."

"You mean, give up being superheroes?" the Blade asked with disbelief.

"Why not?" I said. "It's kind of fun being a normal kid."

"But what about the fame?" Slime Boy cried. "What about the power? I don't want to give those up."

"I say we start a new League of SuperDudes with <u>me</u> as the leader," the Blade declared.

"You? Why you?" Slime Boy demanded. "I'm tougher than you and a whole lot braver."

"Oh, yeah?" the Blade said angrily. "Prove it!"

Soon the two superheroes were rolling on the floor, throwing punches at each other. Their masks fell off and their costumes began to rip. Pretty soon they didn't look like superheroes at all.

"Pretty lame," Toolbox said, watching them. He pulled off his mask and smiled at me.

I removed my mask and smiled back. "I'm tired of keeping my identity a secret," I said. "I'm tired of fighting too. Being SuperKid was pretty cool, but I just want to be a regular kid for a while."

Casey glanced at the Blade and Slime Boy. They were sitting on the floor, covered with cuts and bruises, shouting at each other. They weren't superheroes anymore. They were just plain old Spencer and Ernesto, and they looked really dumb.

"Let's get out of here," Casey said, holding out his hand.

I took it as we left the warehouse together and walked boldly into the sunshine.

THE END